Penelope Wilcock lives in Hastings, in England's East Sussex. Her books explore the Christian faith in both fiction and non-fiction, and are all written with the intention of deepening faith in the reader, and making the Lord Jesus known and loved.

She is author of more than 20 books including *The Hawk and the Dove* series, *100 Stand-Alone Bible Studies*, and *Relinquishment*.

THE HAWK AND THE DOVE, SERIES TWO, VOLUME 2

Brother Cyril's Book

PENELOPE WILCOCK

Hastings

First published 2023 through the Independent Publishing Network
for Humilis, Hastings, UK.
Email: humilishastings@gmail.com

Copy-editing: Louise Stenhouse
Cover and text design: Jonathan Roberts
Cover illustration and typography: Alice Wilcock
A CIP catalogue record for this book is available from the British Library.

ISBN: 979 837427 839 2

By the same author

Fiction

The Hawk and the Dove Series One

The Hawk and the Dove
The Wounds of God
The Long Fall
The Hardest Thing to Do
The Hour before Dawn
Remember Me
The Breath of Peace
The Beautiful Thread
A Day and a Life

The Hawk and the Dove Series Two

This Brother of Yours
Brother Cyril's Book

The Clear Light of Day

Short stories

Thereby Hangs a Tale

Poetry

Urban Angel
(with Stewart Henderson & Ben Ecclestone)

Non-fiction

Spiritual Care of Dying and Bereaved People
Learning to Let Go
In Celebration of Simplicity
The Wilderness within You
100 Stand-Alone Bible Studies
100 More Stand-Alone Bible Studies
52 Original Wisdom Stories
Equality is Biblical
Into the Heart of Advent
Relinquishment

Another book was opened . . .
the book of life.
Revelation 20:12 NIV

Abba, I belong to you.
Brennan Manning

For Alison Day
my long-time friend – with love.

Contents

Acknowledgements and Introduction

A story could just live quietly in one person's heart for ever. To make it useful in the world, so that it can come to life in many hearts, requires a team.

I am so grateful to Tony Collins for his editing and for bringing this story into the public space, to Louise Stenhouse for her highest quality copy-editing and formatting, to Jonathan Roberts for his skill in the patient and meticulous work of getting the text and cover ready for publication, and to Alice Wilcock for her beautiful cover design. Without this team, the story you are about to read would have stayed right here with me. They brought it to you, and I am so thankful to them.

I also owe a tremendous debt of gratitude to my friend and fellow writer Debi Peck, author of the superb book on Religious Scrupulosity OCD, *The Hijacked Conscience* (published by SacraSage Press in February 2023), for reading my manuscript with particular attention to Brother Felix's story, and for the generosity of her warmth and encouragement.

This second *Hawk and Dove* series will all be part of my experiment in gentle fiction, intended to lift up people who have been traumatised, or are highly sensitive, or just very tired and disillusioned. Here you will find no tension or suspense, only a group of people walking quietly and with great determination in a way of life patterned on kindness, understanding and love. To write these stories is, for me, both an envisioning and a prayer – saying that the world can be like this if we want it to be; and may it come true, may it be so. It is written to heal and encourage, to restore and comfort your soul.

Chapter One

When he first came to St Alcuins, Rufus O'Conaill had never thought too much about his name. He had red hair, as did his entire family – he had an older brother with a bushy red beard, three younger sisters with flaming red hair that cascaded all the way down to their hips, and he himself had the pink skin with summertime freckles that complemented his own mop of red hair.

He lived in the village down the hill from the monastery. Though his father attended Mass at the parish church – because it was the obvious place to go, being near and easy – his mother Róisín loved the atmosphere of the abbey. She liked the spacious church, filled with different kinds of light; the golden, slanting light that made Solemn Vespers feel as if it had been soaked in honey, the eastern light that filled the sanctuary with ethereal peace at First Mass, and the shadows that closed around you, morning or evening, in the deep days of winter. She loved the singing, especially the polyphony of High Mass. Best of all, with a special place in her heart, she held dear the brothers of the community. Róisín was only an ordinary village woman, of course, so she didn't really know them well. They were quiet people, enfolded into the purpose of their own lives, the mystery of prayer and the devotion of daily work. Apart from when she went to confession – the prior, Father Francis, was her confessor – she rarely had occasion to speak to any of them; but she watched them, and she loved them, even so. And when he was a little lad, holding his mother's hand, naturally Rufus went there with her.

Robin O'Conaill – Rufus's father – was a stone mason. He regarded his sons as natural apprentices, and passed his skills on to both of them. They learned how to hold the chisel, how to split a stone, how to shape it and how to cut letters into it. But Robin taught them also about the soul and the voice of stone – how slow and deep it is, so that you yourself have to slow down and go deep if you want to touch it. A man must be quiet and observant, must find his own stillness, to have even half a chance of hearing the voice of stone, of feeling his way to its soul. And when he does, he discovers that, unexpectedly, it has a resonance of light. It's not all what you might think, about moss and mud and heaviness. It encapsulates and holds beauty and memory, the thoughts of the earth and the pictures she keeps in her heart.

Robin O'Conaill's sons divided between them the strands of their father's thinking. Rory became an excellent mason, first proficient, then competent, then highly skilled, content in the work of his hands; but Rufus was different. He carried on going all the way up the hill to St Alcuins to Mass – First Mass when he had to, but High Mass if he could get the time off, for the music. He would sit on one of the benches at the back of the nave, looking at the light and the stone, the stone and the light, listening for the soul of the place, straining the ability of his soul to hear the music that lay beneath and wrapped around the music the brothers were singing, the beautiful harmonies they wove to fill the air. He listened for the song of the stone. And when he found it, he felt both honoured and afraid, because it was calling him. That's how he came to be St Alcuins Abbey's newest postulant. That's why he came.

Not once in his time as a postulant did his sense of calling waver – how could it, arising as it did from the soul of the very stones that shaped and held the common life? And at the conclusion of his time, Rufus is invited into the abbot's house to discover the name that will be his when he makes his first vows; his name in religion. As it turns out, this name shapes his path onward, though not quite in the way he expected.

"What do you know about Cyril of Alexandria?" the abbot asks him. Rufus says, "Not all that much, Father," because he thinks that sounds better than "Absolutely nothing," which could also reflect badly on Father Theodore, his novice master, whom he loves.

The abbot smiles because he can read that sub-text perfectly well, and says, "Find out a bit about him when you have time, because you'll be bearing his name."

Brother Cyril? All right. Rufus has heard the name before, of course, and makes plans to visit the library and find out what he can about the man – was he a bishop or something? – whose name he will bear.

But before his good intentions have even a chance of being carried out, Rufus returns to the novitiate room above the kitchens in the eastern range, where his brothers in religion are keen to hear what name he has been given. That's when it all begins to go wrong.

Brother Philip, named after the apostle, whose full profession is imminent and who is known for being something of a wit – or at least, as Rufus's father would have said, "a wag", immediately responds by laughing. "Cyril the squirrel!" he exclaims. "My God, isn't that perfect!"

And it sticks. The strength and impetuosity of Cyril of Alexandria's fiery nature becomes as nothing. The devotion he bore to the Theotokos fades away. His insistence on the integrity of the divine being of Christ is immediately lost. His steadfastness in refusing to condemn the teacher of Nestorius is forgotten. It's just Cyril the Squirrel where it used to be Rufus the Red. Rufus wonders if, after all, learning to ever like Philip again will be the labour of his life. Will he ever learn to shape the stone it leaves in his heart into something beautiful? Will it ever sing or bear a soul, or will it just be there like a lump of granite, the hardened form of accumulated resentment and intense annoyance? Cyril the Squirrel. Thank you, Philip. Thank you so much.

His first response to this is that his entire life is ruined, doomed, and will never be worth living again. Rufus doesn't see how his dignity, the possibility of being taken seriously, will ever recover from this *one comment.*

When their novice master hears of this – and nobody knows how, but he always does, he certainly has eyes and ears, that man – he is quietly furious. He does what he can to remedy it, making sure to include in their novitiate circle teaching about St Cyril's legacy to them in shaping and safeguarding the doctrine of holy church; but he knows his influence in this matter is limited in its scope. He has a pastoral duty to Philip the Wag as well as to Cyril the Squirrel, so after some thought he lets it be. It's really down to Rufus to make the best he can of the path allocated to him. He wonders whether to mention it to the abbot but decides spreading such a thing could only add to the humiliation. Besides, things have an odd way of reaching the abbot's ears all by themselves. He does, though, in a quiet moment, close his eyes and talk to his master about it. "Jesus, my Lord, for heaven's sake, you died beneath an inscription intended to mock you, naked before an audience of people jeering at you. What is there about this you don't already know? Please, beloved Lord, don't let this rob Rufus of the joy of his calling. When he is clothed and takes his new name, please will you walk ahead of him along a path of resurrection. Because of this, may something better come. Please."

The novice most recently received and clothed before Rufus arrived was Brother Ignatius, named for the great patriarch and martyr Ignatius of Antioch. Because he is almost as new as Rufus, a bond of friendship has formed between them, and he has become the person Rufus most often goes to with his troubles. Brother Ignatius is a quiet and gentle soul, and a good listener. He already knows about Cyril the Squirrel, because he was there when Brother Philip said it.

he others laughed, not because they are unkind but because it was ınny, but Ignatius merely bent sideways and downwards to open the ook of Hours beside him on the bench, as a means of momentarily ithdrawing himself from the conversation. He didn't take issue with – because what could he have said? – but it was apparent to him the ıstant it was said that this would be hurtful, and would steal some of ıe joy from what should have been left to be special.

Rufus saw, and appreciated, Ignatius sidestepping the general ıirth, so he seeks him out to confide in him, asking, "Can we go for walk?"

As they stroll along beside the river together, Rufus confesses, I feel as though something's been snatched out of my hands, like a ift taken from me before I even got the chance to open it. When the eremony of my clothing and naming happens at Chapter on Thursday, ıe others are just going to be covertly smirking, aren't they?"

Ignatius says nothing, because he thinks that's probably true.

I can live with it," says Rufus, "not least because I can't see that I ave a choice. It's not so much the ceremony that bothers me. It's more ıat all day and every day, from my naming until my death, I'll be yril the Squirrel in everyone's mind – just a figure of fun."

Ignatius still can't think of an adequate reply to this obvious reality, o he just keeps on listening and walking.

"What can I do, Ignatius? How can I recover my dignity? What can do to make people respect me? People look up to Philip, don't they?"

"I'm not sure they do," says Ignatius quietly. "I think it's more that hilip looks down on them."

Rufus is taken by the insight in this remark, and falls silent himself s they walk up the riverside path. He can't shake this off, though. fter a while, he says, "What would you do, Brother Ignatius, if you anted to earn people's respect and regard – if you wanted them to erceive you as someone to be taken seriously?"

Ignatius frowns hard, considering this question, not one that's ever entered his mind before. Then, “I think,” he says, “I’d probably work hard to excel. In a situation like this, where I’d been stuck with notoriety for some fatuous remark making a demeaning association I’d think my best bet would be to rise above it by being known for something else. I don’t think I’d try to get back at Philip by making him look bad, or by trying to outdo him. To be honest, I think I’d give him a fairly wide berth and hope he either improves or leaves before he makes his solemn vows – which is very likely, isn’t it? This place seems to have an odd effect on people. They change. That’s the impression I get anyway – I mean, do you know even one brother in full profession who’s as much of an idiot as Philip? No? Nor do I.”

“I’m meant to forgive it, I guess,” says Rufus with very apparent reluctance.

“Probably. When the time comes and the edge of it’s blunted a bit. But in the meantime, if you work on excelling at something so much that it becomes the thing people think about when your name comes to mind, I’d hazard a guess that might go some way towards fixing it.”

“Well right now,” says Rufus in a distinctly despondent tone, “ work in the kitchen, and help Brother Richard with the laundry, and sometimes Brother Peter with the horses. In what sense can I possibly excel at doing laundry or holding a horse’s foot between my knees while Brother Peter changes a shoe? And I wouldn’t even want to try and compete with Brother Conradus in the kitchen. If ever there was a man doing the job he was born for, it has to be him. He’s a genius. So, excel at what?”

They are quite a way along the path by now. They’ve gone by the copse and the field adjacent to the burial ground, and got almost to the edge of the farm. The river is shallower and narrower here, splashing playfully over the rocks, the water glinting in the afternoon sunshine.

“Shall we turn back?” says Rufus. “They’ll be ringing the bell for chapel before long, I should think.”

Ignatius feels dissatisfied with leaving the difficulty unresolved like this. As they begin to wander back down the hill, he racks his brain for something that could help. He considers his own name, the gravity and consequence of Ignatius of Antioch – what he did, why he was so venerated. Then he deliberates on Cyril of Alexandria, and why people remembered him – for arguing mostly, he thinks, but decides that wouldn't help. Then he has an idea.

"You know," he says, "the reason we remember Bishop Cyril and Bishop Ignatius, is that they were both writers. If they'd helped do the laundry or muck out the horses, that might have been very useful at the time, but no one would have cared. For all we know, they might have done and it just wasn't remembered. Not many people are highly regarded for doing something useful, but if they write a book, well, that's special, that's important, that makes people look up to them. Why don't you do that, Rufus? Why don't you write a book?"

Rufus looks at him as if he'd lost his mind. "About what?" he says. "I mean, I can literally write – I can form the letters, my penmanship's not awful. My spelling isn't perfect but it's not bad either . . . at least . . . er . . . I guess you could not be able to spell something and not realise it . . . so . . . well, anyway, never mind that. But you have to have an idea to write a book, don't you? Possibly more than one. Isn't the whole point of writing a book that you have something in your head in the first place – something to say?"

Brother Ignatius can think of no reassurance to offer on this score. A book can be boring – and many of them are, as he is finding out. A book can be abstruse. Just because someone's had an idea that doesn't make it a good one. But yes, he supposes that is the nub of it really. A book needs to have *something* to say, be it ever so slight and irrelevant. That's true.

"Well then, I just don't know," he says lamely. They reach the cloister just as the bell begins to ring for None. "I'm sorry, Rufus. I hope you manage to come up with something."

In Thursday morning's Chapter meeting, Rufus sets aside his

layman's garb, and is clothed in the habit of the order, beautifully stitched by Father James. He is tonsured by Abbot John, and given his name. From now on, for the rest of his life, he will be Brother Cyril. The small grins of his brother novices do not escape him as he returns to his seat.

That night, as he goes to his cell when Compline ends, he's still thinking about Brother Ignatius's advice, that he should find somewhere to excel, something for which he could be known and esteemed. That he should – ha-ha, yes, why not? – try his hand at writing a book.

In the silence and solitude of his cell, by the light of the lone candle, he kneels down at the prie-dieu to say his prayers, then makes the sign of the cross on his breast, removes his sandals and pushes them tidily under his bed. He takes off everything except his chemise, and dons his night habit, folding up his day clothes ready for the morning.

He pulls back the sheet and blanket and lies down on the uncompromising resistance of the monastic bed. Even through the linen bag of the mattress and the linen sheet on top of it, the straw is scratchy sometimes. He doesn't mind, though – the one he had at home was no better. He lies on his back in the almost dark, his arms bent and his hands folded under his head, thinking . . . thinking . . . Cyril the Squirrel, for heaven's sake.

It's then that he has his idea. What if he wrote the book of his community? The book of the men of St Alcuins Abbey? What if he got permission to talk with every single one of these men, and asked them four things – what have they learned, what they would like to achieve, what they would like their life to be about, and what they would like their last words on this Earth to be? If he wrote a book like that, it wouldn't just mean that he'd be remembered himself – they *all* would! It would mean that in years to come, when illness or old age had brought their lives to a close, every single one of them would have their own pages in his book. They would not be lost. They would always be remembered.

Brother Cyril, as he now is, knows that self-congratulation is to be avoided, but surely you have to evaluate, have to consider the worth of a course of action before you commence it. And, he thinks, even if his spelling is not entirely perfect, even if he gets some of the letters the wrong way round, surely this has to be a good idea?

A feeling of excitement and contentment begins to glow inside him. He'll need permission to use the parchment and the ink of course, and to talk with some of the brothers in full profession, but he can't see why Father Theodore wouldn't let him do it.

As his eyes drowse shut, he feels purely happy. He's not bothered about red squirrels at all any more. This idea has entirely gripped his imagination.

Chapter Two

As the relentless clanging of Father Bernard with his bell jars Brother Cyril from sleep, his mind – only half here – grabs onto the advice of the novice master that they get up immediately ("just a few moments more" is fatal), flings off his blanket and swings upright to sit on the edge of his bed. He fumbles on his sandals and his belt, struggles into his cowl and scapular, runs an experimental hand over his now faintly bristly tonsure (they are shaved once a week, on a Saturday morning), and stands up to start the day. Already he can hear the sound of feet passing the door of his cell. How do they get dressed so fast? He tidies his bed, folds up his night habit, and joins the community on its way down to Prime.

All through the Office and the Morrow Mass, and while he's washing and cleaning his teeth and breaking his fast with bread and ale, Cyril's mind is entirely preoccupied with his book, in a rising tide of excitement that almost amounts to euphoria.

He waits impatiently for the morning lesson to end, and asks the novice master if he can come back after the midday meal to talk about something. "Yes, of course," says Father Theodore. "Don't forget to let Brother Peter know, if you're meant to be down at the stables this afternoon."

The very minute he's taken his bowl and ale mug to be washed, and seen his novice master leave the frater, Cyril hastens in the direction of the novitiate to wait for him there. Father Theodore smiles, seeing the novice's happiness and excitement writ plain in his face, as he comes in to join him.

"Father, I've had an idea," says Brother Cyril, "but I'll need your permission to do it and also to have some writing things in my cell."

Theodore listens carefully as Brother Cyril expounds his plan. "What are the four questions you're thinking of asking?" he says. When Cyril tells him, he nods thoughtfully. "I love this idea," he says. "What a wonderful and worthwhile thing to do. Yes, of course you can have writing things in your cell – and we can carry a scribe's desk up there for you. Can I suggest that you write out these questions on a piece of parchment, one for each man, with a space for him to write under each question a word or two to jog his memory? If you give them out in Chapter, everyone will have a copy of what you plan to do, and be able to think it over. Yes? I'll let Father John know, so he can make time for you to do it in the morning."

"That'll be a lot of parchment to use all in one go," says Cyril, rather worried.

"Tear each piece in three, and write small," Father Theodore says. "We've got plenty. They'll have some scraps in the scriptorium you could beg, I should think. Tell Brother Cedd you have my permission to take some ink and a pen."

Brother Cyril can hardly believe it is that easy to begin. All it takes is someone who understands, someone who has faith in him and says "yes", and wants to encourage him, in a world where most people most of the time say "no", and want to substitute their suggestion for your own idea. He can't remember when he ever felt so happy. He couldn't care less about being Cyril the Squirrel any more, not now he's going to write a book.

Father Theodore, somewhat to Cyril's surprise – he doesn't learn this until he goes up to the scriptorium to get his ink and parchment when he's finished in the stables – seeks out and asks Brother Philip (specifically) to take a scribe's desk up to Brother Cyril's cell. He offers no explanation and he offers no help. Philip just has to carry it all by himself. He tells Cyril this with a distinctly injured air. “What do you want it for, anyway?” he asks. “You aren’t a scribe.”

There’s no point in keeping quiet about it because they’re all going to find out at Chapter in the morning in any case, so Cyril tells him. “I know; but I’m writing a book.”

Despite the pronouncedly sceptical expression on Philip’s face Cyril can’t help going on to share eagerly the project he has in mind.

“Four questions?” says Philip. “The same four questions to each man in the whole community?” Cyril nods in affirmation.

“What will you do if most of them give you the same four answers? I guess you could group them together, but it would make it a very short book.”

Cyril looks at him in dismay. This never crossed his mind; but once it’s said, he can see it’s a distinct possibility. Their minds and patterns of thought are formed in community by the doctrines and teaching of holy Church. Of course they’re all going to think the same thing – aren’t they?

Philip grins as he sees the horror dawning in Cyril’s eyes. “And anyway,” he adds, “How are you going to remember what they say when you talk to them? They might go on and on about it. You can’t write that fast, can you? What if you forget what they said?” He looks askance at Cyril, who can think of no answer to this. “Well, good luck,” Philip says, in a distinctly dismissive tone of voice. “I lugged that desk up to your cell. I hope you still need it.”

* * *

When it comes to the business of the day after the abbot speaks to the chapter from the Rule, Brother Cyril’s mouth goes dry. He should never have suggested this, it’s a rotten idea. But the abbot’s eyes rest upon him, so understanding and kind, and he explains that their newest novice plans to write a book – one that will put on record for ever the hopes and dreams of the community, the way they saw life, what mattered to them, the men they were. He makes it sound as special as Cyril first imagined.

Abbot John explains that they will all be given the questions written down, with spaces to note what comes to them as they wait for Brother Cyril to find the opportunity for personal conversation. He invites Cyril to give out his little sheets of parchment. Cyril tries to breathe calmly and stop his hands shaking as he stands up to do this. Despite what the abbot said, he feels so scared now, in case it all comes to nothing and he's left looking a complete fool. He goes round the circle of men, and one by one they take the pieces of parchment he holds out to them, each with murmured thanks or a nod of acknowledgement. He sees them beginning to read the questions that he wrote out so carefully and laboriously, yesterday evening in his cell by candle light.

As he gives a sheet to Brother Christopher from the infirmary, the man sitting next to him – the older monk from the infirmary, that man who only recently joined them, the rather intimidating one with the scary eyes – reaches forward and tugs at his sleeve. "Give him two," says that monk. (What's his name? Is it Wilfred? William?) "Brother Michael will need one as well."

Brother Michael, often detained by things in the infirmary that simply cannot be left, is not there in the chapter house. So Cyril gives Brother Christopher an extra sheet. There's something about the tiny encounter that gives him hope. Evidently the monk with the scary eyes sees this as something that matters – that Brother Michael would want to have a part in. Perhaps . . . by this time Cyril hardly dares to believe in what he's started . . . but perhaps he will be able to see it through after all. Perhaps it will be the beautiful thing he hoped. He realises only time will tell.

* * *

"I don't know where to begin," Brother Cyril admits to the novice master. "Who should I ask first? Shall I start here, in the novitiate?"

"I think maybe not," says Father Theodore. "It might take your brothers here a while to dig deep enough – well, some more than others, maybe. It's your book, not mine, so really you'll have to follow your nose, but I think if I were you I might start by writing down my own answers to the questions, and then put them to one side and return to them right at the end. It'll be interesting to find out if your book changes you. Start with the men you work with, maybe? Start where your feet take you. Make a time to see Father John, so you can ask him. It's always possible that men will seek you out themselves, but more likely you'll have to go and initiate a meeting. No one here is pushy; they usually wait to be asked, not out of indifference, it's meant for humility. Actually, one of our most reflective people, and very approachable, is Father Chad in the library. Why don't you start with him? An auspicious place, surely, to open a book! Leave the novitiate until the very end. Maybe – if you like – we can share our thoughts in the teaching circle here one morning. But, Brother, these are only my humble suggestions; I cannot emphasise enough, this is *your* book, so the decisions are yours – not mine. I've never written a book."

* * *

At first Brother Cyril is surprised to find he's the only person – apart from Father Chad the librarian – in the library. He'd assumed it would be busy in the afternoon, when the morning's work is done and men have some time to study. But on reflection, it occurs to him that he wouldn't be here himself if he hadn't come to talk to Father Chad, and a lot of brothers are tied up with the last (and very important) requirements of getting the wheat all in and winnowed, the straw safely stacked in the dry. As well as that, the weather is still pleasant, but next month will bring the wildness of the St Jude's storms, so in this tail end of mellow weather, many men opt to take a book down to one of the carrels in the cloister.

"Welcome, Brother Cyril; what an exciting project!" Father Chad smiles at him and invites him to sit at one of the tables. "And you say I'm the first brother you've come to? What an honour! That makes me feel privileged indeed! Ah – Father Theodore suggested me, you say? Oh, that explains it! He probably thought you should start off with something easy. I'm not the deepest thinker, as you're about to discover."

Something in his manner takes the tension right out of the whole thing, and Cyril begins to relax. For a while this morning he went into complete panic about how he would remember what was said to him, but now he cautiously hopes it will be all right. In the course of his life he hasn't read many books, and hasn't needed to write anything down apart from lessons at school; so he's good at remembering things. He doesn't need to have them written down. Even so, there's something about Father Chad that makes him feel confident he could come back later to check he got it right. This looks promising.

Father Chad has the list he was given at Chapter, and smooths it out on the table to consider the questions Cyril wrote on it.

"What have I learned? Oh, my goodness, Brother – *there's* a good question! I've been thinking hard about this. Some people would say 'not much', I suspect, but I have learned some valuable lessons.

"I've managed to reduce it to just two things. The first thing was a rather bitter pill for me to swallow. I've learned that I'm a shallow kind of man. I'm neither clever nor brave, I'm not mystical and my intellect is pitiable – I'm distinctly slow on the uptake. I like life to be peaceful and quiet. I like to be comfortable and warm and have something nice to eat. I like to be safe. I am nothing special, and I have no depth. I've learned that. But I doubt if that's worth putting in a book. The second thing might be. I've learned that you don't need to be deliberately cruel or evil to do great harm. That you can hurt someone badly by simply failing to see their point of view. Lack of imagination is enough. In connection with that, I've learned – more slowly than should have been necessary – that one can be very similar to someone who presents very differently. It's possible to mistake another person's hopes and dreams as quite different from your own, when they are more like you than they first seemed to be. People can surprise you. Taking the time to see their point of view, finding the common ground, seeing that they are only human, just as you are yourself – I think this has been the greatest lesson of my life. And, I confess to you, I learned not by getting this right, but by getting it terribly wrong. By misjudging. I caused great hurt by ascribing motives and intentions where they did not belong. I should have seen we were brothers in so many ways. I can't say more without giving away stories that are not mine to tell. Is it all right if I leave it there? Yes? You're very kind.

"Now, what about your next question. What would I like to achieve? I must be careful, mustn't I, not to muddle that together with the question after – what I would like my life to be about – because I see that though they are similar, they are also different. That's very discerning of you, Brother Cyril."

He stops, and frowns at the paper, blows out his breath as he thinks. "Dear me. I think the chances of my achieving anything whatsoever are slimmer than you might be hoping. I . . . well, this really comes from the thing I told you I'd learned, how much you can hurt someone by failing to understand them. And what I'd like to achieve, if I could have a free choice, would be . . . er . . . to play a full part in making our house here a place of refuge; so that other people like me – even the ones who don't at first appear to be like me – men who long for peace and quiet, somewhere welcoming and safe, can find in our abbey a reliable shelter from the storm. If I could do that – not all by myself of course, we all have to work together – then I think I could say my life had been worth living. Is that all right? To offer those desperately in need of it some shelter from the storm? Yes?" He looks up at Cyri from the questions on the table before him, and nods.

"And the third question: what I would like my life to be about. I suppose, being the librarian, you might expect me to be all taken up with philosophy and theology, but I'd have to disappoint you. I . . . well . . . I think if my life had a *story*, as it were, it would be about the wonder and the power of being given a second chance. About what a grace it is to be offered an opportunity to start again . . . with someone. That, above all else, is what has changed me, given me hope, forged friendship. The gift of a second chance. Does that sound all right to you?

"On to the fourth question then – what I would like my last words on Earth to be. Goodness me. I suppose that would depend on if I was alone or was with someone, if I died suddenly or had some time to reflect. It would be rather circumstantial, I suspect. But I know what you mean. D'you know, Brother Cyril, I don't think I really have a great message to leave or teaching to pass on. Not if I'm honest. If our abbot was at my bedside, or if I was simply alone with my Lord, either way I think what I'd really like to say to them is, 'Thank you.' For what, I suppose you want me to say. I'd want to say thank you for firesides and summer days, for the truly precious gift of a quiet, uneventful life, and for the understanding of the ones who had the humility to hold out to me the chance to try again, to make a new start. 'Thank you.' That's what I'd like to say. Is that . . . is that all right, Brother? Does that bear any resemblance at all to what you were hoping for? I hope it's helpful. I hope I haven't been too verbose for you."

One thing stands out very clearly to Brother Cyril; he will need to go *straight* to his cell – *straight there* – and write this down, before he loses the flavour of the simplicity and humility that has moved him so much in what Father Chad said to him.

"That's perfect," he says. "That's just perfect. Please forgive me, please excuse me, I need to go and write it down. Before I forget, before I lose it. Don't say anything more to me, Father, I've got to get that written down. Thank you so much!"

He scrambles to his feet, grating the chair on the floor (for which he apologises), and heads for the door. Looking back, he sees Father Chad is chuckling, understanding the urgency of his haste. So grateful that the library is only just round the corner from the dorter, so nothing intervenes before he can get into his cell and shut the door, he carries what he has heard into the privacy of his room. He sits down at the desk that Philip has stood under the window for him, picks up the quill pen and opens the pot of ink. To his great satisfaction he remembers it all with absolute clarity, and gets everything onto the page just as the chapel bell begins to call the brothers to None.

* * *

Having served them his masterpieces in light, airy, ever-so-flaky pastry for their supper, Brother Conradus can't help noticing they've left the frater liberally sprinkled with crumbs. He apologises to Brother Cyril, saying, "I know you do need some time to relax, you poor lad," but courteously asks him nonetheless to go back and wipe down the refectory tables carefully and thoroughly, while Brother Richard sweeps the floor. He says he knows everyone has mice, but he sees no need to offer them such liberal encouragement.

Brother Richard looks up from his sweeping as Brother Cyril comes in with a bowl of water and a cloth. "Oh, thank you," he says. Then he adds, "Hey, while you're here, do you want to know my answers to those questions you left us? Or do you have to be sitting at a table to write it all down?"

Cyril smiles at him. He likes Brother Richard, the fraterer, and their paths cross often. "I remember," he says, "I write it up later."

"Righto, then," says Brother Richard. "Straight in? Well, I thought something I'd learned is that it helps to have a system. When you're fancy-free and living on your own without a care in the world, you can do what you like when you like and hope to get away with it. Not here. If the cloth doesn't go back on the right nail, if the broom isn't in the corner where you expect to put your hand on it, if the Mass settings aren't stacked in order and set out ready, it all goes wrong and tempers get frayed, and suddenly we aren't sweet-natured and holy any more. Someone can't find their saw or the shears, and they're cursing and swearing and calling you all kind of names in the silence of their heart – and then they have to confess it at Chapter and you sit there feeling wretched because you know whose damned fault it is really. I mean, think what would happen if our infirmarian put the hemlock in the wrong jar, and sent his assistant to fetch a sleeping draught for one of the old men? He might sleep for ever! Order, a system, discipline; it's necessary.

"What I'd like to achieve? Well, frankly, *anything* would be good. But here's something. The fraterer's work, Brother, is . . . how can I put it . . . boring? I get bored, and my mind sinks down to a mundane level. I get obsessed with wax polish and counting the cutlery. What I try to achieve is working on two levels simultaneously; making sure I fulfil what's asked of me, but also staying in prayer, in the presence of God. That makes me sound more saintly than I am – the point I'm making is exactly that I don't achieve this most of the time. My aim is to persevere.

"Ah, Brother – when you asked what we'd like life to be about, I got a kind of feeling as if I started out in the entire cosmos, out in the stars or something, then came zooming in to the here and now. What life is all about, whether I like it or not – and I'm talking about monastic life now, I don't know about anything else – is practical detail. People think here in the abbey it's all silent meditation and ascending prayer and wafting incense, and yes, we do a fair bit of that; but it rests on a bedrock of look sharp, sit up, pay attention and think what you're doing. Weeding the garden, scouring the pots – *making* the pots to scour – tending the sick, polishing more wood than you imagined a building could possibly contain, kneading mountains of dough scrubbing acres of floor, mending drystone walls, keeping account – Brother, this is monastic life. It's practical. When you get that right oddly, you create the space for the soul to fly free and the prayer to ascend. There's a paradox in it, that the humdrum, tedious, everyday round of work lays the foundation for building a holy life.

"My last words? I think that depends on how I die. But whatever they are, I'll do my level best to make them something grateful something godly, something kind. I mean, it would be a shame if the last thing I did was swear at the man who inadvertently severs my jugular vein while he's sharpening the knife to carve the capon. So to speak.

"Do you mind tidying that last one up when you actually write it Never mind about the swearing and the capon; I only mean I hope I'll leave something kind and thankful on the air, with my last breath."

Chapter Three

Brother Cyril picks up the stack of dishes left tidily on the end of the table in the frater at the conclusion of the midday meal and carries them through. The servers are wiping down the tables and will bring through the fruit bowls and ale jugs before they take their own meal in the kitchen. He takes the dishes into the scullery and sets them down beside the big sink, then goes back for his apron. He's just put it on and tied the strings when Brother Conradus comes through with the big bowl of dirty spoons in his hands.

"Thank you, Brother Cyril," he says. "I can wash these up – Father Francis wants to see you. He said he'd be happy to just stay there in the frater until you're done, but better not to keep Father Prior waiting, eh? I'll wash up. I think he wants to talk with you about your book – as I do myself. I loved your questions! I keep turning them over and over in my mind. I've already decided on five completely different versions of what my last words on this Earth will be! Bless you, Brother, don't worry, we can finish up here – off you go."

So Brother Cyril obediently takes his apron off again, hangs it up and walks back round the cloister to the frater, to find the prior. Francis is sitting at one of the long refectory tables, holding the piece of parchment with Cyril's questions in his hands, reading them.

Brother Cyril has this in common with everyone who comes to St Alcuins, whether a monk or a visitor – he really likes the prior. Father Francis is courteous, cheerful and friendly, he never takes offence, he puts people at their ease, and his smile charms even the most hard-bitten and cynical of souls. He was one of the people who welcomed Brother Cyril when first he arrived, and took him to meet the abbot, chatting amiably as they crossed the abbey court, making sure Cyril arrived at Father John's door feeling relaxed and confident, his initial trepidation laid to rest – well, relatively so.

Since that day, because Brother Cyril is only a novice and Father Francis is not only a monk in full profession but one of the senior brothers, Cyril has had very little to do with him. He notices him in chapel, finding his place in the breviary, settling to quiet reflection with his eyes closed, listening with thoughtful attention to the abbot's homilies and Chapter addresses. He sees him at meal times in the frater, very self-contained there, with a kind of *inward* air, as though he somehow vanished into himself when they sit down to eat; but nonetheless always alert to the needs of his neighbours when they need someone to pass the ale jug or the butter dish. Occasionally Father Francis stands in for Father John when the abbot is detained elsewhere, taking his role in the prayers of the community, or sitting at his place in the frater. Only very recently Father John went away to Whitby for a week's retreat, so with journey time he was away for a fortnight. Father Prior presided over the Chapter meetings during that absence, and for the first day after the abbot's return to let him get his breath back before resuming his responsibilities. Brother Cyril enjoyed those Chapter addresses – they were intelligent and thoughtful, full of wit and humour; not irreverent but very funny sometimes. The prior has a way of being able to make people smile. Observing him around the abbey, Brother Cyril sees a gracious, unassuming man, quiet but with a sprightly step and a twinkle in his eye. He has an indefinable sparkle about him, yet dignity with it, somehow. In truth, though, Cyril hardly knows him at all, so he counts it a privilege to have this opportunity for conversation that might not otherwise have come his way for a long time. He's looking forward to the chance to know him better.

Father Francis, quietly mulling over the questions, looks up as he hears Brother Cyril approach and smiles at him. Cyril immediately and involuntarily smiles back. It crosses his mind that there are those who might say Father Prior is wasted on monastic life, that any one of thousands of young women would have fallen head over heels in love with him just for the charm of his smile. And they do; Father Francis is used to adroitly fielding undisguised admiration from most of the ladies who visit the abbey. He knows how to receive their enthusiasm with friendly courtesy that affirms them as human beings – and leaves it there. On the receiving end of the prior's smile, Cyril sees why they settled him in that obedience; what an asset he must be to the interface between the community and the outside world. And within it, the petty differences that seek to harden into entrenched antagonism would have a tendency to evaporate, he thinks, if you talked them through with a man who smiled at you like that. He has good teeth, too.

"Thank you for doing this," says Francis, the friendliness of his gaze engaging Cyril's as the novice takes his seat across the table from him. "It will be very uniting, I think, for us all. And your questions will make us review why we are here and where we're going. Genius! Well done! What would you like me to do? Just launch in to my thoughts? Do you need to write anything down?"

"No, I write slowly," says Cyril. "It's made me quite good at remembering. But I'll show you before it's bound, in case I get anything wrong."

As the prior takes this in, and nods, and looks again at the questions, Brother Cyril thinks how nice it would be to have a friend like this man. He wonders about friendship inside the community. Father Theodore has talked with the novices – he does this with every new intake – about the implications of their vow of celibacy, that it is not about renouncing carnal knowledge only, the act of coitus, but about attachments and preferences, about what is called particular friendships, where you get very close to another individual in a way that separates you out as a pair, or as a small group, from the common life. Their commitment to celibacy is a witness to the open vulnerability of the love of Jesus – that it is for everyone, nothing held back and no one left out. Even so, Cyril thinks, there must be some people you like better than others, some who understand you and some who completely baffle you. There must surely be people who scare you and people who bore you – mustn't there? And people like this man, with whom you'd just love the chance to be friends.

"Your first question," says the prior, looking at the sheet of parchment, "asked what we've learned. D'you know, Brother, I have found these questions extraordinarily difficult! They look so simple and yet I find the answers to them surprisingly elusive. As though they are there, but behind locked doors inside my soul, and I have to wait patiently outside until they open. Then, when they do, I get more than I bargained for.

"So this first one, I started off thinking, well, let me see – what have I learned? And after about fifteen minutes, I thought . . . heavens . . . what *have* I learned? Have I learned *anything*? In the end, I could only think of two things, that belong together. Am I allowed two? If not, I'll tell you which is the most important one.

"I've learned not to pretend. When I came here, I depended heavily, without realising it, on charming people and pleasing them, on kind of . . . er . . . *seducing* them into liking me. I was afraid of abandonment and rejection; it's a long story, it has to do with my childhood in part, but not entirely. I felt unworthy, and ashamed of being me. I was afraid of being unacceptable, of being cast out once I was seen for what and who I am. I was frightened that I'd be found wanting and go to hell. I felt afraid that I would lose the good opinion of the community around me if they saw me for myself. I felt . . . erm . . . I think 'untouchable' might be the right word. Or maybe 'unclean' something like that."

Brother Cyril listens to this with frank astonishment. He has seen the playfulness, the merriment, in the prior's eyes. He has watched the man's jaunty step as he crosses the open space of the abbey court. He has seen him chatting with people, seen the laughter that drifts out from any conversation he's involved in. What he's just said could not be more unexpected.

"It took me a while, and I needed – and got – some help, but I did manage to find my way to the level of self-acceptance where I could stop pretending all the time; stop acting, stop . . . um . . . manipulating people, I suppose.

"But that was secondary. This is what I mean about two things – I'm sorry to take two! Because the thing I've really learned, that made it possible for me to stop pretending, is that I am loved.

"That has arrived in my life along a variety of pathways, love kindly and humbly and honestly held out to me; but most of all I found it when I realised that in the place of abandonment and exclusion, on the margins, in the wilderness if you like, Jesus already is . . . erm, I mean he's already there. And I know, I can feel, that he loves me. And that's what I've learned. I didn't know it before I came here, and even once I was part of the community I had to travel down a long track before I found him. But he's there, and he loves me. So, I've learned that I no longer need to pretend, because I am loved just as I am."

He nods, thinking about it. "Is that too wordy? Will it do?" he asks.

"Thank you," says Cyril. "It's perfect." And the prior smiles at him.

"So . . . your next question is – no, wait – there's something more about what I've learned. To do with loving and honesty. I spoke about being loved, but there's also the loving. To make it work, what I've learned is not to grasp, not to be possessive or exclusive. To have no particular friendships. Every time my hands want to grip and clutch, to open them again – and again. Even if I quite desperately want to keep something for myself, to open my hands and let all of it be for everybody. If that makes sense.

"Then, that next question is – I'm rambling, aren't I? I'm so sorry, I'll try to be more focused – what I'd like to achieve. Goodness me . . ." He pauses in what he's saying, gazes at the scrubbed wooden surface of the refectory table where they sit. *If someone could only teach Brother Richard to eat with his mouth shut,* he thinks, *that would be accomplishment enough for a human life.* But obviously you can't say that to a novice, even as a joke, which it only half would be. Leaving pretence behind is one thing; shattering a person's ideals, even when those are illusions, is another. "You know," he continues then, "what I just said to you? Well, it occurs to me that other men could very probably also give the answer that here they've learned to accept and believe they are loved. If that happens, and you don't want duplication, feel free to drop it, won't you? It will be enough to say that here I learned to stop pretending; the people who know me well will understand.

"What I'd like to achieve . . . can we . . . is it all right if we come back to that? May I go on to what I'd like my life to be about? Because I find that easier to answer. Perhaps if I speak about it, then I'll be able to identify what I need to achieve if I'm to bring it into reality . . . if you see what I mean.

"What I'd really like my life – our life here, lived in community – to be about is inclusion, acceptance maybe. That's what the practice of Benedictine hospitality is, at heart. I know we can't take in everyone who wants to join, sometimes it just doesn't work out or they haven't understood what we're trying to do. But every now and then, here, there comes somebody who has been rejected, who has lost self-respect, self-esteem. We . . . very occasionally we've had someone who . . . er . . . hasn't a good reputation. There may be a resistance to letting them try the life. There may be an instinct to shut them out. When such a person gets involved with us, it inevitably means we're in for a bumpy time; a lot of pastoral work for our abbot, a great deal of re-evaluation and adjustment to be done throughout the community. But I'd like to think we have enough faith and wisdom to be able to work with such a man, when it happens. I'd like our community here to be a circle of healing, where people who haven't been able to fit in anywhere can find a place to belong. To make it like that requires inner work from *all* of us but also from *each* of us. I'd like my life to be about helping that happen.

"Thank you for letting me answer that one first, because now I can see that it has indeed taken me back to your second question – what would I like to achieve? And I'd like to cover that distance I described – to do the soul work necessary to allow me to accept others just as they are. After all, if I learned that I am loved, and that I could stop pretending, does that not give me the responsibility to extend the same healing and hope to other people?

"And then, you asked about my last words . . . My mother died when I was very young, Brother Cyril. I think it's fair to say that a lot of my struggles may have stemmed from that – not all, by any means, but many. I loved her so much. My father was a good man, but rather distant. When we speak of God as our Father, I have to confess it doesn't do for me what it's intended to. It creates no sense of warmth or closeness, intimacy and trust. It just speaks of authoritarian control – and even, if I'm honest, an association with betrayal. My father married a woman who was not very kind to me. I wasn't grateful, though I hope I did my best.

"So . . . when I – in my private prayers, you know – I most often call God 'Mother'. It makes sense to me; my mother *is* in heaven, and I loved her so. At the very end, when it's time, when I've finished whatever it is I came here to do – and I hope that will be what I just said, the creation of a community of healing acceptance – I think . . . in my heart at least . . . my last words might be, 'I'm home, Mother! I'm home!' But . . . oh, God, Brother Cyril . . . is it really advisable to actually write that down in a book? That's stopping pretending writ large, is it not? Oh, go on, then. Let me just say it. I've had enough of trying to fulfil expectations."

He looks at Cyril, and again he smiles, but in his face the novice sees something sensitive, something brave. "I hope . . . oh, never mind," he says. "Pick out of it all what you think is helpful. Leave out what you judge is best forgotten."

As he climbs the day stairs to his cell, to write this down before he forgets, Cyril thinks back over the encounter. He wonders if it's not perhaps rather unusual for someone in so senior a position as the prior to have the grace – or maybe the uncertainty – to entrust a novice with the task of deciding what to reveal and what to enfold into silence.

Opening the door of his cell, he sees a small sheet of parchment has been pushed under it into his room. It's one of his sheets of questions. At the foot of the page where they're written, someone has penned, in perfectly even script, the words "see over". Then the other side is entirely filled with neat, tiny writing. He wants to read it, but deems it wiser to first set down what he's remembered from talking with Father Francis. He fills a sheet with notes, and by the time he's done that the bell has begun to ring for None. He's so curious about the page awaiting his attention that he takes it to scan through quickly under the light from the window, even though he knows he's risking being late for chapel. It says – the lettering so impeccably clear that he can read it easily despite it being minute – "LEARNED ~ that I am missing something. So far I cannot identify it. I know I am a sinner, steeped in iniquity, but I cannot find the way to peace I see in our brethren. I haven't got it right. TO ACHIEVE ~ Purity of heart, a move towards personal holiness, integrity greater than being merely correct, meaning that lies deeper than facts and informs them, look past history to eternity. I aspire to rectify my priorities. In the interest of accuracy, it is Fr. Theodore who pointed me in this direction: I did not see it for myself. I aspire to be pure in heart. WHAT MY LIFE MIGHT BE ABOUT ~ righteousness not just precision: a prophetic life not merely pedantic. Truth in the inward parts. MY LAST WORDS ON

EARTH ~ Hide thy face from my sins, and blot out all mine iniquities. Create in me a clean heart, O God; and renew a right spirit within me. Cast me not away from thy presence; and take not thy Holy Spirit from me. Please pray for me. Pax. Felix."

Then, if he really squints he can read the minuscule script running up the side of the text in what space remains, the narrowest of margins: "I hope this meets your requirements. Br. F."

The bell stops ringing. Brother Cyril hastily puts it down on his desk, pushing it half under the stack of notes already there so it can't be wafted onto the floor, lets himself out of his cell and runs down the stairs as fast as he can. He slides into his place in chapel, breathing hard, just as the abbot gives the knock and the community rises. He's not late, then, strictly speaking, but he can see his arrival lacked decorum and he will have to apologise. He should not have dallied, as well he knows. As Father John begins the opening responsory, clear in his mind Brother Cyril can picture the page of text he's just been reading through, in such faultless lettering except near the end there was a mark on the words, blurring the ink. He knows what it is, it's happened to him often enough. It's the watermark you get when a tear falls on the page. *How very odd*, he thinks; *I wonder what that was all about*. It's a good thing – isn't it? Surely? – to get things right? To be holy? That lettering was immaculate, and the spelling too, as far as Cyril can judge. But it lingers in his mind that Brother Felix asked if he would pray for him. This feels like an honour, and a trust. He resolves to do so. Every day.

Chapter Four

"*Stop it*," someone says, quietly but with a considerable degree of severity. "Stop rushing. Do it calmly. Do it slowly. Do it properly. What's the matter with you?"

Brother Cyril, standing outside in the passageway with his hand raised to knock at the door, isn't sure what to do now. He lets his hand sink to his side. In the whole time he's been at St Alcuins, no one has spoken to him anything but gently and kindly, with remarkable courtesy. This, a lot more blunt, sounds as if someone's being told off. It must be really bad. To be honest, he hadn't expected it in the infirmary of all places. He's had no reason to come here before, and during his months as a postulant the routine enema and bath was not yet required of him. This morning is the first time Father Theodore has sent him across to see Brother Michael for that purpose. There were some old monks dozing in chairs out in the garden. He hesitated over the possibility of asking them where he'd find Brother Michael but they didn't look as though they'd be all that helpful. So he came in through the open door, glancing into the empty frater and continuing to the next room, where he heard slight sounds of movement and was just about to knock.

As he stands there wondering what on Earth to do, a monk – the one who told him to give an extra sheet of parchment to Brother Christopher – comes into the doorway carrying a tray of tiny cups and bowls, evidently with some kind of medicines in. He stops, seeing

Brother Cyril standing there. "Oh, hello," he says, fixing him with a very unnerving gaze. Brother Cyril recognises the voice he just heard from inside the room.

"I was looking for Brother Michael," he says nervously.

"Ah, yes – for an enema? He'll be over in the bath house getting ready for you. D'you know where it is? I can show you in a minute, if you like; I'll just put these in the frater ready to be given out. I've no idea where Brother Christopher is – he's probably making beds."

There are, Brother Cyril has been told, three infirmary brothers. So if the other two aren't here, who was this one talking to? He stands back to allow him through into the passageway, and risks a look into the little room – oh, it must be the dispensary – before following him. There's no one in it. Only then does it dawn on Brother Cyril, the monk must have been talking to himself.

"You – you do know me?" says the infirmary brother, re-joining Brother Cyril in the passage after dumping his tray of doses on the table in the frater. "My name's William."

"Thank you," says Brother Cyril. "I wasn't quite sure. Although I should have remembered. It's only that there are so many names and new faces to take in. But I should have known because I was here as a postulant back in the summer when you asked for admittance, in Chapter."

"Oh. Yes. Of course," William replies, in a not especially encouraging tone, leading the way out of the main building and round to the bath house. "There you go – that's where you're headed. You'll find Brother Michael inside."

"Thank you, Brother," says Cyril, politely. William wonders whether to correct it to "Father", and decides not to bother. He nods in farewell, and leaves the novice to his own devices.

Brother Cyril feels distinctly nervous about this health procedure, but Brother Michael's gentle friendliness sets him at ease. As he lies on the sheepskin padding in the stone bath while Brother Michael runs the herbal tisane into his gut, the infirmarian says, "Thank you for the questions you sent, Brother Cyril. Brother Christopher and Father William brought a copy of them across for me."

"Oh, no!" Cyril stares at the granite wall of the bath, embarrassed. "He's a priest, and I called him Brother. When I met him just now. I didn't say 'Father.'"

Brother Michael laughs. "He wouldn't mind about that," he says. "William's not the kind of man to get hung up on status." He wonders whether to add, just to be reassuring, that William probably wouldn't even have noticed, but knows that's a flat lie, so decides against it. Instead he says, "I liked your questions. I've given them a lot of thought."

"D'you want to tell me your answers to them?" the novice says, eagerly. "I don't have to write them down, I won't forget."

"Well," says Michael, "this is the first enema we've done for you, and you've not had one anywhere else before, so maybe not right now. One thing at a time. This is your chance to rest and cleanse and be peaceful. Come back and have a proper conversation with me . . . er . . . not this afternoon, we're a bit busy; and tomorrow will be frantic. The day after tomorrow maybe, after the midday meal and before None? Will that work for you? Yes? Good. There we are. That's all run in nicely. Are you comfortable? Yes?"

He leaves Brother Cyril to rest quietly while the tisane cleanses his blood. *This whole enema thing is very odd*, thinks the novice, *but what a nice man Brother Michael is*. As he lies there, he begins to plan out who to see next. He decides to try and talk with the brothers who work on the farm, after None today. And then maybe Father James in the robe-making room tomorrow. That's only two doors away from the novitiate, he might get the chance to look out for him coming up after Chapter, and make a time then.

* * *

"Brother Cyril," says the infirmarian as Cyril comes out of the bath house feeling clean and relaxed from the luxurious novelty of a bath, "can you do me a favour? I'm meeting myself coming back today, there's just so much to do. Have you time to run these accounts and lists of what we need across to Brother Cormac in the checker? I'd be so grateful. They need the abbot's signature still, but some of the requirements are urgent – he'll understand."

As he's missed a significant chunk of the morning lesson, and the time it takes to have an enema and a bath is hard to estimate, Cyril thinks he won't be in trouble if he fails to report back to the novitiate straight away. So he thanks Brother Michael for his ministrations in the bath house, and takes the sheets for Brother Cormac through the cloister and out into the abbey court to the checker.

The cellarer is on his own in the checker, going through a stack of chits kept on a spike, with notes of what various monks have taken from the stores for the places where they work. He takes the documents from the infirmary held out to him, gives them a cursory glance, adds one to the pile of request lists and gets up to tuck the other into the infirmary book.

"Have you got a minute, Brother Cyril?" he says, as he comes back to his seat behind the big table covered with notes and account books. "Yes? Pull up a stool, then. D'you want to hear what I thought about the questions you gave us for your book?"

If there's one man at St Alcuins as unnerving as Father William in the infirmary, in Cyril's opinion it has to be Brother Cormac in the checker. Everything about him looks wholly uncompromising. He wonders if Father Theodore was actually expecting him back before the midday Office – he hadn't anticipated this – but he doesn't dare raise any objections. Obediently he fetches the stool and sits down by the table.

"D'you want some paper?" Brother Cormac asks him. "To write notes, I mean." Cormac has recently persuaded the abbot to let him send for a packet of that paper made from old sheets or something, that you can get from Norwich. He's doing his best to introduce it at St Alcuins instead of parchment, for anything not requiring a permanent record. He's been wondering if they couldn't even learn how to make it themselves. Paper is what he's given Brother Cyril for the first draft of his book, though obviously he'll need parchment – if not vellum – to write the finished manuscript out in a fair hand.

"No, I'll just listen," Cyril says in reply to his question, wishing his voice didn't go so reedy when he's feeling nervous. "I can remember."

He's relieved that the cellarer looks down at the pen he's picked up and is fiddling with; Cyril doesn't think he could meet that ferocious blue gaze for long.

"You asked what we'd learned. What did you mean? I still haven't learned how to do all the administration. I still need William to come over and help me from time to time. I was the kitchener a long while, since I first took my vows until I was moved to this. I thought I'd learned to cook, but now I've seen what Conradus can do I've reluctantly had to admit nothing could be further from the truth. And if I encountered any temptation to doubt that, my good brothers have always been happy to set me straight. Apart from the obvious things like reading music and finding my way round the breviary, and Greek and Latin, I don't think I've learned anything. Possibly not even that."

He glances up at the novice, who clears his throat. "I . . . um . . ." Cyril doesn't want to sound rude. "I maybe didn't ask the question very clearly. I'm sorry, that must have been unhelpful. What I had in mind was – er – like, the path your soul walks on. You know – sort of, life lessons more than skills."

Suddenly, unexpectedly, Cormac grins at him. "I'd wager you anything you like, if you ask whatever monk you first meet when you walk out the door, what life lessons has Brother Cormac learned, they'd just laugh at you." He doesn't sound bitter or cynical – just as though he thinks it's funny. Cyril wonders if the whole conversation vill go like this, and he's glad he saw Father Chad and Father Francis irst. It gives him confidence.

Brother Cormac looks down again at the pen in his hands. His air grows round his tonsure in wild, tousled curls, greying now but vidently once black.

"Well, life has taught me to let go," he says. "I . . . my mother died in shipwreck – I've no idea who my father was, or if he was with her, or vhat. I was very small. I don't remember it clearly. They said I clung to er as if my life depended on it, which no doubt it did at some point. But she was dead. So I had to let go. Someone took me in and raised ne; they were good to me, but I didn't really . . . well . . . fit in. So they rought me and dropped me off here, and I had to let go of them. here are some things that are very important to me, but not all of hem can be accommodated here. I've sometimes tried to find a way o sneak them into the life here, but it's been made very plain to me hat I'm under obedience; I have to let them go. When I was a novice, I vorked in the infirmary for a bit and then in the kitchen. God, I hated ur kitchener with a passion. We nearly came to blows. But our abbot ook the time to show me how to see things differently, how to let that o. Over time, I came to love him – Brother Andrew, our kitchener and then he died. I had to let him go but I clung stubbornly to the itchen work even though everyone tells me frankly I'm a lousy cook. ventually, when Conradus showed up, Abbot John moved me, so I ad to let it go. Taken all in all, I dare say that's the main thing that's ome up in my life over and over again. I should think it's what I came ere to learn, wouldn't you agree?"

"That sounds . . . sad," says Cyril.

"Aye, well it's been a struggle at times, but maybe I shouldn't hang n so tight to what I care about. Maybe I have to move on from being wo years old and shipwrecked. Perhaps that's what it's all about. That person can let go – it's safe to do so. Life goes on."

Here it is again, Cyril thinks. *Such courage, such honesty.*

"I – what was the next question? I'm sorry, I've got the sheet you gave me somewhere, but as you can see, there's quite a lot of notes and letters and whatnot festooned around this shack. I'm not quite sure where I put it, now. Oh – I might have left it in my cell."

"It was what you would like to achieve," says Cyril. Cormac looks at him and starts to laugh. "*Me?*" The more he thinks about it the more he laughs. Cyril isn't sure how to respond or what to make of this, so he just waits. And eventually the cellarer says, "God bless you, Brother, both for the entertainment and for having the wild imagination to think I'd be achieving anything. Candidly, I'm just grateful they let me stay here and are prepared to put up with me!" His gaze challenges Cyril with genuine merriment.

"Well," says Cyril, "what – er – what would you like me to do, then? Just leave that one out?"

"No," says the cellarer penitently. "No, I'm sorry. It's important to you, isn't it? Well, all right then, what I'd like to achieve, I can't. I've tried everything I know and it's just thrown back in my face. The thing above all I would really like to achieve is for human beings to offer animals compassion and respect. Not kill them, not eat them, not keep them trapped in filthy pens, not beat them and kick them and take their children from them. I wish we were born with fur or feathers, and then maybe we'd get a better grasp on the reality that we are the same as them. We are animals too. We depend on mercy and kindness. Why can't we pass it on? Let them be free, let them be happy, see them as our sisters and brothers, *help them*, for pity's sake."

This is completely unexpected. When the cellarer looks at Cyril his eyes blaze and flash. Then, "People just think I'm crazy," he says. "'Yes, Cormac, but you have to be realistic.'"

"Is that," Brother Cyril asks him, "something else you've had to let go?"

When the cellarer looks at him then, Cyril is astounded by the depths in his eyes. "No," he says. "It's not. I will never let it go. It's what I believe in. I don't care what religion teaches, I think they've got this wrong. It's my personal belief that the Creator who made all the life on the Earth and called it good and blessed it, and entered into a covenant with it, expects us to treat it with the same seriousness, the same reverence. So I just do what I can, what the abbot will allow me to do. And yes, I know he turns a blind eye to what others might say he should stop me doing. Feeding the wild creatures and suchlike. I'm not ungrateful. But if I could realise my dream it would be like the holy mountain the prophet Isaiah described – where nobody would hurt or destroy any more, and wars would end, and the animals live in peace. Actually, I'm very thankful this is *finally* going to be *written down*. It's high time somebody did." He looks at Cyril very carefully. "So? Do you think I'm crazy now?"

Apart from anything else he might think, it feels like an honour to be spoken to as an equal by the brothers in solemn profession – as the other men he's spoken to also did; with no pretension, nothing patronising, no built-in reminders of the difference in status – as though Brother Cormac thinks of himself only as a person, not as a Somebody.

"Not crazy, no," Brother Cyril answers him. "What you just said makes perfect sense. But, unusual, I think. And I can't see how . . . Well, what would we eat if we didn't eat the animals? What would we wear without leather and fur and wool?"

"I don't know," says Brother Cormac. "But I do know this: all the while we aren't giving it any thought at all, we'll never find out. Anyway, leather can wait until they die of old age, eggs we can have because the hens don't go broody on all of them, milk we could just take a little extra while the mother has a calf at foot, wool we can take without hurt to the sheep. We could do all these things and be kind, be gentle with them."

Brother Cyril can see he's given this some thought. "Thank you," he says. "If you hadn't put this to me, I would not in a thousand years have thought of it for myself."

Something in the cellarer seems to relax, to soften. "What was your next question, then?" he asks.

"It was what you would like your life to be about."

Brother Cormac blinks. "About? How d'you mean? I . . . my life isn't *about* anything. I'm just me. That's what it means to be alive – in the image of God, you know, I Am That I Am. Something that's about something else isn't a person, isn't alive, but just a tool, with a use derived from whoever uses it. The whole point of a living being is that it has no secondary purpose. It's primary. It's holy."

Brother Cyril had not thought of this as a possible response. "Surely, though," he ventures hesitantly, "we – er, it's – that is to say – don't we live in the light of something greater than ourselves? Isn't that what it means to live with reverence?"

Brother Cormac considers this. "Yes. I suppose. I mean, it's not that I think I'm God. Well, that is to say, I *do*, but I don't think all of me is all of God. I think I . . . well, like a wave has the sea in it, and that's what a wave is, God is in me. But there might be other things in me than just the ocean, I guess – a floating turd or two, or at least a drift of tangled seaweed. And there's certainly more to the ocean than just me waving."

Brother Cyril thinks he might be losing the thread of this. "So . . . what would you like me to put, when I write it down?" he asks.

"Oh, well, fair enough," says Cormac. "Let me think. How about you say that my life is about really becoming who I really am? Fulfilling the potential of what God intended in me. Will that do?"

"Yes," says Brother Cyril, grateful it became that concise. "Yes, that's perfect."

"There was another one, wasn't there? Weren't there four?"

"Yes, the last one was what you would like your last words on Earth to be."

"Oh, well, that's easy," says Brother Cormac. "I can manage that one. It would be, 'Please, if you loved me at all, *please*, for me if not for them, don't forget to feed the crow and the fox and the mouse under the woodpile, and the garden birds.' I'm quite certain about that. And I might have to add, 'I'm sorry I've left such a muddle in the checker', because I do get a bit behind, but though that's true I wouldn't bother writing it in a book, if I were you."

He looks at Cyril. "Is that it, then? Oh, damn, there's the bell for chapel and I'm not half through this lot. Never mind, I'm quite certain it'll wait for me."

"I'm sorry to have taken up your time like that," says Brother Cyril as the cellarer locks up the checker and they walk across the court together to the west door of the church.

"Oh, you can come back whenever you like," says Cormac. "No one else ever apologises to me. You're a novelty, Brother, a complete one-off."

No, I'm not, you are, thinks Cyril, as they walk into the silence of the church. Though obviously he doesn't even consider actually saying it, not only because they should be in silence here but because it would be inappropriate and outrageously cheeky to say such a thing to one of the senior brethren – even one with a style as markedly informal as Brother Cormac's.

Chapter Five

When the Office of None finishes, Brother Cyril walks up the hill with the farm brothers through scattering showers of half-hearted rain. The grain is all in and threshed, so the mood of urgency that seized them in the last few weeks has gone. They have all read Brother Cyril's questions and are in a cheerful, talkative mood. There would usually be four of them, because the novice Brother Nathaniel has been allocated to the farm work, but this afternoon he has to practise refectory reading with the precentor. So today there are just Stephen and Damian and Placidus. They're happy to share their thoughts. Brother Cyril hopes he'll remember everything they said – harder when you're talking to three men than just the one, but he will do his level best to commit it to memory.

Brother Stephen thinks that apart from learning the essential skills of assessing grain and thatching ricks and castrating pigs and birthing lambs and milking cows, the main thing he's learned is that the glory of God shines through to him in the beauty of the land and the sky. The hills, he says, hold light as if it had been caught in a bowl as it poured down from heaven.

Brother Damian says he's learned that he's not cut out to be a schoolmaster. When he was a boy he helped his father, who is a farmer. Mostly he liked working with the sheep – and his sister kept her own little herd of goats. He likes animals because they're simple; dealing with them is natural and straightforward. He likes to feel the wind on his skin, the sun and the rain. Since he was moved from the school to the farm for his work at St Alcuins, he's learned all over again how grateful, how blessed it feels, to be out here on the hills, with the scent of heather drifting from the moor.

Brother Placidus says he's learned to work together with others – that as a boy he was always so shy and solitary, rarely noticed and almost never included. He's learned here what it's like to join in, for people to make space for you without question; to have a place.

When it comes to what they want to achieve, they seem strongly focused on what is immediate and practical. Brother Stephen is thinking about drenches for the ewes and getting the tups in to the sheep shed ready for mating. Brother Damian is planning to have everything ready for them to start ploughing next week. Brother Placidus has been soaking hazel and oak to make baskets, along with some willow withies that he was allowed to buy in from the land at Tadcaster. They need more apple baskets, and he's thinking if the rain sets in he could make himself useful starting work on those. Brother Cyril tries to imagine all this included in his book, and thinks, why not? It gives as good a picture of life at St Alcuins as anything.

Their life, all three of them are in agreement, is about simplicity and faith, the interweaving of the chanting of the Office and the farming day, the agricultural seasons of the light and the round of the church year. It's all the same, they tell him. The infant light born in the depths of winter and growing from there, the issuing forth of life rising again at Easter, the feast they've just had of St Michael and All Angels warning them to prepare their bodies and souls against dark days.

And their last words? Brother Placidus has no idea. He thinks if his soul was required of him tonight, he'd be thinking about that verse in the Psalms that speaks of the autumn rain clothing the land with blessings. Brother Damian says he hopes his last words will be from the Shepherd psalm – "Though I walk through the valley of the

shadow of death, I will fear no evil: for thou art with me." Brothe
Stephen smiles, and just says, "All is safely gathered in."

And then they reach the farmyard and make it courteously clea
they want to get on with their work. But Brother Cyril has what h
needs. He thanks them, and makes good haste to get back down th
path to the abbey buildings, in through the cloister and up the stai
to his cell, so he can get all this written down while it's still right ther
fresh in his mind.

* * *

Brother Cyril is just about to pick up the supper dishes neatly stacke
on the end table, when he feels the lightest touch on his elbow. Turnin
he finds himself looking into a pleasant and gentle face. Diffidence, h
reads, but also an indefinable strength. "If it is a good moment," th
monk says, "may I talk with you about your questions? Will here, i
the frater, do?"

Brother Conradus, tipping left-over fruit into one bowl an
stacking the emptied ones, looks across and nods at him. As the mon
goes to sit down again on one of the vacated benches, Conradus come
past Cyril with his bowls, all the fruit piled in the top one. "Yes," h
says. "I'll get the crocks."

"What's his name?" murmurs Brother Cyril.

Brother Conradus has mastered the curious monastic skill
speaking perfectly distinctly for his hearer, yet so quietly as to b
inaudible to anyone else. "Brother Germanus," he says. A small impis
grin flashes briefly as he looks at Cyril. "Don't worry, in no time at a
you'll know us better than you ever could have wished. On you go."

He sails off into the cloister passage with his tottering stack
bowls and fruit, and Brother Cyril crosses the room to meet Broth
Germanus. He can see this man would be easy to just not notice. H
is as unobtrusive a person as you could ever imagine. He sits dow

opposite him, and Germanus says, "Hello. Good to have a chance to meet you properly. How's everything going? Are you settling in well?"

Brother Cyril nods in affirmation, and says yes, he's loving it. He feels a definite appraisal in Germanus's gaze. *This man*, he thinks, *really sees me.*

"Good," says the monk. "Well, your questions, then. You asked what we've learned. I presume you mean *something* we've learned, otherwise this book of yours is going to weigh a ton!" He smiles at Cyril. It doesn't sound sarcastic, just gentle and humorous. "One of the best things I've learned," he goes on to say, "is that you can choose what to see of a man – the outside, which is quick, easy and obvious, or the inside, which takes longer and more effort of perception. Every time – I mean, *every* time without fail – the inside is nicer than the outside. It's worth the effort. Maybe . . . if you could learn that too, it'll be helpful. But perhaps you already knew, and I'm being presumptuous.

"Then, what I would like to achieve, you asked. Well, something I've tried to learn, then I drop the ball and I have to start over again, is not to take things personally. If someone upsets me, I try – and mostly fail – to understand that what I'm seeing is about them, not about me. I think, Brother, it will be the work of a lifetime for me. I'm quite touchy by nature. I'd like not to be.

"Of what life is about, again, this is absolutely vast, isn't it? Like, how long have you got? I presume you mean us to pick one aspect. So what I've chosen, because it's huge, it's really important in monastic community, is that what privacy and peace we enjoy is a gift we offer one another. Custody of the eyes and ears, you know. There's what you can't help noticing, but from it you make a deliberate choice what to hear and see. You decide what to signal you know, and what to just fold into interior silence. If you took that away, there'd be mayhem; we couldn't do it. Seeing, not seeing, hearing, not hearing – never abandoning someone, but giving him privacy; leaving him not loneliness but peace. It's an art, and it's massive.

"And my last words. The thing is," Germanus says, with a rueful smile, and looks down at his hands resting on the table, "I'm completely chicken about anything painful or frightening. I don't want to go to purgatory, let alone hell. But if I gather the courage to look at it steadily, I can see that Christ is the best judge of me – not myself. He knows me better, he sees past my evasions, my small deceits, the ways I flatter myself. So I'd like my last words to be – in principle, even if I cannot frame them – 'Do with me what you will, my Lord.'

"And I want to say thank you, Brother. I have to say, very rarely is anyone interested in my opinion, and it's hardly surprising. To be asked what I think is a rare treat." He grins, suddenly, and Brother Cyril gets a glimpse into his lightness of spirit, a man who doesn't take himself too seriously, but who has self-possession and dignity nonetheless.

Brother Germanus, I hope I can find the grace you clearly have, he thinks, *to grow into what it means to be a monk. Properly.*

* * *

As he comes out of his cell, having written up in a fair hand some of the notes he has made, heading for the novitiate fireside because his hands are so cold – the evenings are chill, now – he sees two young monks sitting in the dusky light on the top step of the day stairs. It's Brother Christopher and Brother Cedd. They look round as they hear footsteps coming along from the dorter. "Hello," says Christopher. "We thought you might be up here. We were waiting for you."

Brother Cyril comes to join them. The stairs aren't really wide enough for three, unless you squash up close, so he goes down past them and sits sideways on the stair a few steps below.

"Brother Felix is worried about the note he left you – in case he pushed it under the wrong door, and if what he wrote wasn't what you needed, and in case you were offended that he didn't make the time to see you in person," says Brother Christopher. "He's in the infirmary," he adds. "Came in this afternoon."

"What's happened?" asks Cyril, concerned.

"He . . ." Brother Christopher glances at Brother Cedd, who says nothing. In a very quiet voice, Christopher says, "He's done some damage to his back."

"Oh, what? Ouch! He's had an accident? Did he fall from something?"

"No. Um – no, not that kind of damage. With his scourge. He's done it before, Benedict says. He gets so wound up, you know? In the end he has a bit of a breakdown. He doesn't always do this, though. He hurts his arms sometimes. His wrists. Mostly he just kind of falls apart; but today . . . well . . . don't you ever do it, will you, Cyril? Go easy with the scourge. You can hurt yourself quite badly. He's all right, but . . . erm, it'll be very sore. Brother Michael painted it with egg white and put a green poultice on, and then a bandage. He says it'll heal up in a few days with all that lot slathered on it, but even so, Felix has to stay in the infirmary for a while – partly to make sure it gets properly better, but I guess also to be sure he doesn't do anything else to himself. I think Father Abbot came in to see him just now after I came up here. But, look, keep this to yourself, won't you? I probably shouldn't have said. It's just that Felix was worried about the note he'd left you. Asked me to check all was well and you weren't displeased with anything. That's what he said. What shall I tell him? Was it sensible, what he wrote for you? He can get a bit garbled when he's coming unstitched."

Soberly, Brother Cyril takes this in. "It made perfect sense," he says. "Yes, it was fine, and I was grateful to have it. Tell him I'll put it to one side until I'm done – or until he's better – so he can review what I write before I complete the finished version. Then he can satisfy himself it's what he wants to say. I'm so sorry this has happened. He asked me – in his note – to pray for him. Please will you tell him that I certainly won't forget? Every day, tell him. That is, I don't mean tell him every day, I mean tell him that I'll pray for him every day."

Christopher smiles. "Aye. I will. And we were thinking, do you want to know *our* answers to your questions? Shall we tell you now? With Felix out of the scriptorium and in the infirmary, really quite poorly, there's going to be more to do in both – so we thought we'd come up and find you now."

"Are we . . ." Brother Cyril hesitates. "Surely we're not allowed to sit and talk in the cloister, are we?"

Christopher grins at him. "That's right. We're not in the cloister though. We're on the stairs. And no one's about. So . . .?"

"Well, yes please," says Brother Cyril. "I'm listening. I'm good at remembering. I'll let you check before I make a fair copy. Go on, then."

"Right," says Brother Christopher. "Tell us if we just say the same as everyone else – I expect we can dredge up something different if need be. We have hidden depths. At least, Cedd does. Hidden shallows in my case. Go on, then, Brother Cedd. You're the senior brother."

Brother Cyril notices that Brother Cedd doesn't dismiss this as a joke, though he doesn't look as though he takes it too seriously either. Precedence, he realises, is important in this place. He thinks it's not to lord it over others but just so that life can organise itself and shake down effectively.

"What have I learned?" Cedd muses. "I've been wondering what I should tell you. Because, you know, I very nearly left, Brother Cyril. It was during the time Father William lived away from here. I reached a point where I felt so downhearted, so inadequate, I'd just reached the end of myself. I knew where he was living, and I went to find him. You— you've met Father William, have you?"

"Only in passing. Just briefly in the infirmary," says Cyril. "I know who you mean, but not much more than to say yes, I've met him. He – well never mind; this is your turn to talk. Carry on."

"I think my answers to your questions will mostly trace back to that day I spent in his house while he was out of monastic life. It proved to

›e a turning point for me. What I learned, which is something Father Villiam said but Father Theodore used to tell us, too, is that if we ıotice anything lacking in our community life, we have the option to ry and put it there ourselves. If there is coldness, warm things up. If here's indifference, show people what it means to care. If there's any ·ullying or picking on people, quietly stand by them. Of course, we ·robably wouldn't want to join if it was that kind of community – ·ullying and picking on people, and it's not – I'm only saying these s examples. So that's the main thing I've learned. To notice what's nissing and try to supply it myself. Did you want to say yours, Brother Christopher?"

Christopher shakes his head. "No, I'm enjoying listening to you. Go hrough all four of yours first, then me. That way, if we get interrupted itting here, at least Brother Cyril will have one set all in, instead of wo halves."

Brother Cedd nods in acquiescence. "Oh, yes, that seems sensible. Vell, then, your next question, what we want to achieve, also – for ne – arises from that day with Father William. He welcomed me into is home, he was not unkind, but he was certainly very direct when came to discussing the difficulties I was going through. And not aving it within me to achieve *anything* worthy of note was exactly my roblem. He changed my understanding of it, to being at peace with eing unimportant, being content to be nothing special. He said if I ad been important and special, I'd have had a worse struggle trying ɔ be humble. Ever since then, I made it my aim in life to take the ›west place. Because, as they say, if you sleep on the floor you can't ıll out of bed. One of the surest ways to achieve contentment and eace is to aspire to lowliness in the first place. After all, someone has ɔ be the lowliest and the least, don't they? Why not me? I sometimes vonder if in truth I'm just a bit lazy, don't make enough of an effort, if 'm avoiding responsibility. I can't really tell, but being the lowliest and ne least has become my aspiration in life. Climbing down is easier than climbing up, and it makes one heck of a lot of arguing redundant.

"And what my life is all about? Father William said to me, that day, 'You wanted to join, they let you stay, that might have to be enough.' I've never forgotten it. It was . . . well, not very easy to swallow at the time. But the more I thought about it, the more I could see that way lies contentment. Just to accept one another and accept myself. But that wasn't the main thing. Father William said the point of any life is to encounter Jesus Christ, to walk with him as a friend. You open your heart for him to dwell in; you invite him in. And I did, and it made all the difference. So I'd say he was right. That is what life – any life, not just mine – is about. Making friends with Jesus. I hope that doesn't come across so nauseatingly holy it makes you want to gag.

"Then, my last words . . . well, I hope I would say what Jesus said on the cross, 'Into thy hands I commend my spirit.' I say it every day. I'd like to say it once more, just to be sure, before I die.

"Again, I have to say, I really do hope, thinking over what I've just told you, that it doesn't sound too insufferably pious. I can see it's not very original – not at all, in fact, it all came from Father William. It might be just very religious and rather boring, but hey, that's me. Oh! —" He stops suddenly, his face flushing. "Oh, I didn't mean *Father William* is very religious and rather boring! No, no! You – well, once you get to know him you'll see no one could say that about him. I just meant me."

Cyril looks up at them sitting on the top step, Brother Christopher listening to Cedd, his face amused and full of affection. He can see the friendship between them. Christopher turns his head to look at Brother Cyril.

"Brother Cedd was in the novitiate when I came here as a postulant," he says. "He had the cell next door to mine. He definitely feels like a brother. And don't be deceived by all this self-deprecation. You couldn't find a truer spirit or a kinder friend. My go, then.

"When I first came here, I felt almost as if I was flying, I covered so much ground in so short a time. I saw so much, and all the impressions were so vivid, and to be honest I just loved everything and I still do. But there's one thing in particular I've learned because it comes up for me time and again – I'm quite a slow learner, you see, it takes a few goes round before I absorb it. And it's that there is an immense power in prayer. When you pray, it almost shockingly shifts things. It makes a difference. Over and over again, when I've been stuck or despondent or confused, or come up against something incomprehensible or immoveable, it's when I've finally had the nous to pray about it that I've seen things change. Every time. The outcomes aren't always what you expect, so you can miss what's happened if you get too stuck on waiting for a particular result. But times beyond counting, I'll be sitting in chapel or falling asleep in bed – Ha! Or falling asleep in chapel – and suddenly I see that something I prayed about has changed or resolved. It's . . . I don't mean to sound irreverent, but it's sort of like a game, it's fun in a way. The other thing I learned recently, that I'm massively enjoying, is how to play chess, but I don't think that belongs in a book about monastic life."

He sits on the step, hugging his knees, and says thoughtfully, "What I want to achieve . . . man, I don't really know. If I could one day be as good an infirmarian as Brother Michael is, or Father John, that would do for me. I love the infirmary work. And, what my life is all about? Well, there's real meaning in a name, and my name – Christopher – felt distinctly daunting at first. St Christopher carried the Christ Child across the river. He almost didn't make it, but he managed to get him safely to the other shore. Not everything we do in the infirmary is about dying; we try to make people get better when they're ill, obviously. But a fair bit of it is about helping men to die, to preserve dignity and find peace and calm fear; to carry them safely over the river, and set them down on the other side. It feels like such a huge and solemn responsibility and it's what my life has come to be about. Sometimes, in holy pictures, in icons, they depict a person's soul as a child. How I think of it is having the sacred trust of carrying their soul safely over, like St Christopher carried the Christ Child – and seeing that when I support them and help them, I am carrying Jesus, and Jesus is carrying the world. It's the place I want to stay and never move from. Working alongside Brother Michael, and bearing these beautiful souls across . . . what more could anyone ask?

"But then, sooner or later it'll be my turn, won't it? And I wonder who will carry me? Whoever it is, by that time I'll have done enough of it to absolutely appreciate the joy and the cost and the everyday hard slog of them looking after me. I hope I'm not a heavy burden to carry. I hope bearing me over doesn't cause them to stumble. I hope I can be trusting, and light on their shoulders. But when they get me safely over – and they will, there's no doubt of that – I want to look back one last time and say, 'God reward you,' before I leave."

He looks down at Brother Cyril. "Will that do? Is that the right kind of thing? I don't think I have anything else in my heart, truthfully. That's it."

Chapter Six

"Woah! Will! You're looking distinctly green! Are you all right?"

Brother Cyril, walking along the passageway, hears these words spoken in the infirmarian's voice, confirming that he's in the right place. Out in the garden Brother Christopher told him he'd find Brother Michael in the scullery, and waved vaguely in the direction of this doorway in, but gave no clearer directions than that. *"Will" who? Could he mean Father William?*

Yes, it is Father William. He recognises the voice when he hears the reply. "I managed to slice through two very alive and wriggling maggots, cutting up these windfalls for the men's supper. It's . . . oh, God, it's revolting. Turns my stomach." (That's not all he says, the original is riper, but the expletives are expurgated in consideration of the reader's sensibilities.)

Both of them have their backs to the door, and both turn when Brother Cyril says, "I'm sorry. I should probably have been doing those for you, in the kitchen. Brother Conradus said to come straight over, to see Brother Michael. He says you only have specific times when you're not busy, so he just sent the apples over this morning instead. That's why I didn't cut them up." He speaks humbly, feeling ashamed, and suddenly very conscious of the eyes of both men upon him. Brother Michael's right; his assistant does look more than a little queasy. Cyril adds, "If you give me the apples, Father William, I could cut them up now, and listen to Brother Michael at the same time."

The infirmarian, his face alive with humour and kindness, looks to Father William for his response. The intelligence with which Father William regards him, however off-colour he might be feeling, enters straight into Brother Cyril's soul. He recalls Brother Cedd speaking of this man with such admiration. *This is different from most places*, he thinks. *Nobody ever looked at me like that anywhere else.*

"I'd be so very grateful," says Father William (he sounds as if he means it). "If you can stand it. Thank you, Brother. I'll bring the bowl and the knife out to you – I presume you're going into the garden? It's a nice day. I'll fetch you a cup of ale too – both."

"I could just take the apples with me?" suggests the novice respectfully, and William picks the bowl up, passes it into his hands. "Thank you kindly," he says. "Apples, maggots – all yours. Good luck."

Brother Cyril follows the infirmarian out into the garden, and they sit on the bench under the tree. "Is . . . erm . . . is Brother Felix all right?" he asks, unsure if he's even supposed to know about this.

"He will be," says the infirmarian cautiously. "He – what have you heard?"

"He sent me a message because he left a note under my door with his answers to my questions. He was worried in case his replies weren't what I wanted. Brother Christopher explained that he was here, that he's been . . . um . . . unwell."

"If you'd like to come and see him tomorrow, please do," says Brother Michael. "He'll be here for a few days, I think. He's on the mend. I'll tell him you asked after him."

This sounds like a definite directive to change the subject. Brother Cyril starts to cut the apples carefully, keeping a sharp eye out for maggots, and flicking off any he finds onto the grass. "Can you remember my questions?" he asks.

"I think so," says the infirmarian. "Your first one was asking what I've learned. I'm not sure how concise you want me to be. I mean, I've learned a lot."

"Whatever goes through your mind," Brother Cyril says. "I'll take it all in. If there's anything really specially important, perhaps you might write it down, if you have the time. But I'll show you the pages before the book is bound, so if I get it wrong you can tell me."

"It divides up into three," says Brother Michael. "There are the practical things – how to give an enema, how to rub someone's body to relax them, how to move and lift bed-bound men without hurting them or myself, what medicines to give for what illnesses and in what amounts – all that kind of thing. I learned mostly from Father John, but also from Brother Edward who was our infirmarian before him. And these practicalities shouldn't be underestimated, they also reach people's souls. To be comfortable, to be free from pain and able to sleep, to sort out a boil or an ingrown toenail or a broken bone – my goodness, does it not make a difference to a man's capacity for praying and trusting in God and loving his neighbour! There are few things more spiritual than keeping your bowels open and getting a good night's sleep. So that's the first thing, and I suppose in our community it's what I'm known for.

"But I've also learned from Abbot John things like how to be firm with people, how to really listen, how to love completely without sentimentality, how to go beyond myself when I'm almost too tired to stand up, and still not be snappy or sarcastic, just contain myself and stay calm, stay kind. He showed me how to do that, by his own example.

"Then the third thing I've learned is from watching and listening to the people who have come here for my care. I've learned that whatever happens to you, there is always some spring of grace to be unearthed. However bad it is, even in disfigurement and pain – and trust me, it gets more than gritty at times – there's that in it we can learn from, something to help us grow. I remember our abbot before Father John – Abbot Columba, but we knew him as Father Peregrine – saying to Brother Thomas that he'd learned how to love in darkness, to find the way when there was no light left to show him the path. That's the kind of thing I mean. His soul grew in stature and his light strengthened even as his natural abilities declined and illness confined him. He raged at it sometimes, of course he did; but he shone as well. It's no good moralising at people of course; nobody feeling sick with pain or with grit in his eye wants to hear me saying, 'Everything happens for a purpose, Brother.' He'd probably hit me. But it's a beautiful thing, it really is, to see even the most ordinary of men find their way to the springs of grace in the arid valley. It humbles me, and it gives me hope – because I'll be old too, one day. Is that all right? Is that the kind of reflections you were imagining? I've been thinking so hard about your questions. Mind you, I've forgotten what the next one was, now."

Brother Cyril has almost finished the apples, even though being windfalls they are rather fiddly to do. He cuts into the last one. "Yes, that's absolutely perfect," he says. "And the next question I had was what you'd like to achieve."

"Oh – yes! Of course. That's easy, and short. I want people to be happy. To be comforted and relieved of pain. I want to help them find their way to contentment. That's the sum total of it really. Just that."

The novice thinks how much he likes this man, and how glad he i that writing this book has given him the chance for these conversations

"Oh, thank you, Will," says the infirmarian as Father William come towards them with cups and a jug of ale. He nods in acknowledgment holds out the tray for them to take their drinks, and picks up the bow of cut apples. "God reward you," he says. "I don't know how you ca stand it. Bad enough when *men* have worms – although maybe you' have been in a better place without the benefit of that observation *Mea culpa*, and thank you, Brother."

Worms, thinks the novice, suddenly grateful he works in th kitchen, not here, maggots in the apples or not.

The infirmarian takes a sip of his ale. "Brother Christopher keep this cool for us by dangling the pitcher in the well. Absolute geniu

Isn't it delicious? Now then, you wanted to know what I'd like my life to be about, didn't you? Well, when I first saw your list of questions, what immediately came to mind was healing and kindness – *shalom*, I suppose. To be whole, to be well, to have what weighs us down and hurts us lifted away. And that's true, of course; but then I had another thought – less near to the surface maybe, but equally true.

"You see, it occurred to me that something you *hadn't* asked is what we are afraid of. Please don't get me wrong, I'm not suggesting you *should* have asked that. I can see that the answers to these four questions will amalgamate into a record of what has blessed us and lifted us up, tracing the way we have walked. It will be a beautiful book, Brother Cyril. And you don't want a catalogue of nightmares blocking the light. I think your questions are just right. But I have to confess that the whole of my time here in this community, I've been dogged by a particular fear. Sometimes it hems me in so much that it becomes quite paralysing. I've carried this dread in my heart of a time when contagion could come to England, to us here in Yorkshire, to this house where we have lived in such tranquillity and contentment. I've even dreamed about it sometimes – dreamed of men parched with thirst and covered in boils, racked with pain, reaching out to me and begging me to help them, and I was the only one left, everyone gone. There wasn't enough of me to go round, nobody to help me, no remedy to ease the sickness. And no escape. When I have those dreams, I wake up trembling and drenched in sweat, and I beseech God – absolutely beg him – to spare me from anything like that ever happening.

"But I've come to the conclusion, through those dreams and because of the fear I've always carried, that the thing I'd most like my life to be about is absolute childlike trust – in God, I mean. Because there are going to be times, as even the most cursory consideration will tell you, that I am not equal to the task. Sometimes a man is in agony and our best remedies don't shift it. As I grow old, how do I know what will happen? I might be blind and deaf. I might be incontinent. My joints might hurt all the time and my legs might ulcerate. I can do my best to pursue health, but life does have a way of catching up with us. I can run and dodge and hide, but it'll find me in the end, won't it? And when it does, how do I know who will be here to look after me, by then? Will they be gentle and understanding? Or will they be impatient and scornful and have a nasty cruel streak in their nature? I don't know, do I? I mean, look at Jesus. He helped all those people, and healed them and gave them hope, and taught them the ways of Paradise – and what happened? They flogged him and jammed thorns on his head and hammered nails through his hands and feet and hung him up in the midday sun to die agonisingly as his arms dislocated and he suffocated under his body weight. And they watched, and they laughed at him. I mean – *what?*

"So, the thing I'm working on, quietly in my own heart, day by day – although I suppose everyone will know about it once you've written your book – is learning to trust God absolutely. I want to abandon myself without reserve, to his love. I want to let go of my fears and terrors so completely that I just walk easily and gracefully through this world. Not because everything's all right, but even if it's not. That's what I'd like my life to be about. Is that – can you manage that? Is it too much to say?"

Brother Cyril sits in silence, not sure how to respond. He supposes, now he thinks about it, that if you ask questions like this of a community of monks, they're going to come up with something that challenges you, that puts out a hand and touches the depths of your heart. And this does. "I hope I can find my way to something similar," he says. "It's what would make life worthwhile."

Brother Michael smiles. "I've completely forgotten the last question, now," he says.

"It was what you would like your last words on Earth to be."

"Oh, yes! Well, for me that kind of follows on from what I was just telling you about. You know – of course you do – that the last words of Jesus were, 'It is finished.' I expect you've listened to theologians arguing and heard homilies and read books going into what he meant. I gather it's meant to be, 'It is accomplished!' That the great work of redemption he came here to complete had reached fruition. But sometimes – just in private, this is not edifying – I've wondered if there was also an element of 'thank God that's over' in it. Maybe. And because so many times I've felt afraid, and wondered what the future holds for me, and seen so much suffering and not always been able to help, I've thought my own last words might end up being something similar. 'It's finished.' And I hope, I really do, that it'll have some kind of overtone of 'Yeah! We did it!' Not just being glad when it finally comes to an end. Life . . . it can be very difficult sometimes. The human body can hold one hell of a lot of pain."

He falls silent. The breeze stirs the leaves overhead, and one leaf falls spiralling down onto the wall in front of where they're sitting. "Of course," says the infirmarian quietly, "it's all absolutely insanely beautiful as well. I mean, what a wonderful thing, to have the chance to see a sunrise, to see geese flying overhead, to see the raindrops on a spider's web, to sit with a friend beside the embers of a fire, to be hugged by someone who really, truly loves you; even if . . . well, never mind."

Brother Cyril isn't sure if here he's heard something beautiful enough and strong enough to see him through the rest of his life, or just something so unbearably sad he could cry. He feels that thing happen that he never knew anywhere before he came here, of suddenly shifting into a different dimension altogether, the place where a soul can mature into what it was meant to be. And that it comes at a price.

* * *

Walking down the day stairs in the direction of the abbey church,

Brother Cyril is still thinking over his conversation with Brother Michael. He managed to rush up to his cell and write most of it down before the bell for the afternoon Office began to ring.

He brings his mind back to the here and now, certain there's something he's meant to be doing. His feet drift towards the door, but then Father Bernard is at his elbow, reminding him he was meant to go into the vestry and be shown the vestments and where and how they are stored, as well as where to find all the numerous bits and pieces kept in the sacristy. Father Bernard also intends to show him how to work the thurible. Cyril apologises profusely for forgetting, and as soon as None is over he rejoins the sacristan and follows him through the Lady Chapel into the vestry, where Bernard has some ceremonial items laid ready for the novice to see.

"I've been thinking about your questions," says the sacristan, smoothing the humeral veil he's got out of the drawer on the polished and splinter-free surface of the long chest against the wall. "I liked them. They've provided a lot of food for thought. We use this in Holy Week, when we lay the blessed sacrament in the altar of repose. I'm sure you'll have seen it. Your question about what we've learned made me think. There is so much detail to our life here, and so much emphasis on making sure we fulfil its requirements, that we spend most of our time learning that, and attending to it. But the curious thing is that what we eventually learn is that all the plethora of minutiae isn't what matters at all.

"This is the stole our abbot wears for the Rose Sundays – Gaudete Sunday and Laetare Sunday. Such a beautiful colour, isn't it? I'll show you the chasuble if you like. The first time I began to see it was not the detail that mattered was the point at which it all began to come together as a pattern for me. I started to see the picture, not the pieces. At first what I saw was that it is beautiful. But then I began to see that it is a story – like an illuminated manuscript, that makes you gasp when you open it, because it is so lovely. All this we do, these details with their beauty are the illuminations of the story. But the round of the church year that sets before us over and over again the pain and betrayal, the forgiveness and friendship, the sacrifice and healing, the poverty, the simplicity and humility, the gift of peace, the treasure we hold in vessels of clay – all of it, brought to our minds in a rhythm of repetition by the beautiful detail of what we do here – what I've learned is that put together it tells the story of salvation. It's not actual salvation, for that can only take place in the individual human heart; it is very intimate. But it is the story, that holds out to us the invitation. And if we say yes, it becomes the beginning of transformation. That's what I've learned.

"This stole you will be used to seeing, because it's worn by the celebrant for all the Sundays after Trinity. Here is the Lenten one, and this is the Paschal one – embroidered with thread of gold, look. Then you asked what we would like to achieve. I have a confession to make to you. I get very caught up in self-importance. I am very conscious of seniority, of being a priest, of . . . rank, I suppose. Ceremony means a lot to me, and so does position. I am very proud of being a brother of this house, and not always for the best of reasons. Our abbey is well-regarded. What I would like to achieve is the total lack of pretension I see in Abbot John. I've never known such a down-to-earth man in all my life. If I could achieve the level of honesty and kindness and humility and integrity our abbot has, that would do for me.

"This little set here is kept for when someone comes asking for a visit – the last rites usually, or sometimes if a woman is churched at home after childbirth. Or if a babe has to be baptised quickly. We keep this compact set, with the stole folded with it, because sometimes it has to be grabbed when time is short. There are the anointing oils in these vials, and here are the vessels for the holy Eucharist. Our abbot always allows people to communicate under both kinds, he will offer the chalice even to the laity. There is a sound theological basis for it in holy Writ, but we don't say anything about it to the bishop.

"You asked what we felt our life might be all about. I have been thinking about it ever since you placed the question into my hands at Chapter. I couldn't think of the answer, but in the end I knew why. don't think my life is about anything. It is ephemeral, passing, mortal. It's just a mark on a page, like a speck I might brush away when smooth the surface of the fair linen cloth on the altar. My life is there to point beyond itself. The whole round of liturgy and the rhythms of community, they are there to say, if anything, 'Not this, not this Like in heraldry, where you get gold fleurs-de-lys on a field of blue – and the blue is ground pigment, pure lapis lazuli, a depth of blue that leaves you amazed at its beauty. It's the field of blue, it's the eternity we cannot even understand, it's the Ancient of Days, the unutterable magnificence of holy presence, transcendent, beyond the power of the human mind to grasp. And it is love, it has a heartbeat, it is pure unconditional love. That's the place we meet it. That's what my life is about.

"I'm so sorry, all this talking, I've let the time run away. I'll have to take you through the use of the thurible another day. No, it's not your fault, you can't be expected to remember everything, it's just that I've been talking so much. I'll have a word with Father Theodore to make another time. My last words? Oh, yes, of course. I've always loved the words of the *Nunc Dimittis*. There is something about the sense they convey of fulfilment and satisfaction, that floods my soul with peace God willing, I would like my last words on Earth to be, 'Lord, now lettest thou thy servant depart in peace, according to thy word. For mine eyes have seen thy salvation.' To have seen this, Brother, to have handled these holy things, to have lived in this place with its peace and touched eternity, I have no words for it really. Only that it fulfils me. It feels, you might say, enough."

Chapter Seven

Brother Conradus takes two stools and stands them in front of the fireplace where they have already set the pot of soup to simmer for supper later on. It has some barley and dried peas (soaked overnight) in it, so he wants it to cook through the afternoon over a low fire. He picks up the broom propped against the wall by the door, and lays it across the tops of the stools, thus creating a rail on which he proceeds to hang the cloths wet from drying the dishes. This is because it's raining hard outside; there's no point putting them out to dry in the garden.

"Applaud my genius!" he says with a dazzling smile, swivelling round to face Brother Cyril, closing his eyes, smiling modestly, laying his hand dramatically on his breast as a man humbly in receipt of highest praise. "Not really," he adds. "It's what my mother used to do. Oh, but wait!" He stops dead under force of sudden recollection. "I know you said you had to go and give Brother Peter a hand, but if you can manage *five minutes* before you go, I wanted to tell you my thoughts about your book questions before they evaporate completely – the thoughts not the questions, though you never know."

Cyril loves working with Brother Conradus. In the whole of his life he has never come across anyone so encouraging, so cheerful, and so kind. "Yes?" says Conradus. "Good man! Pull up a stool. Here you are, someone spurned their honey cake. It'll only go stale. You eat while I prattle. Have some butter with it. Have a cup of milk to wash it down. They can be a bit dry on their own."

They've only just finished the midday meal, but Brother Conradus's honey cakes are so very delicious Brother Cyril is immediately in favour of this excellent plan. They sit down by the huge work table with its surface shaped into a landscape of hills and valleys by generations of chopping kitcheners preparing vegetables.

A sudden ear-splitting crash of thunder directly overhead makes both of them jump. "Mercy!" Conradus exclaims. "That was loud. Oh! Glory! There we go again. Heaven help us, that sounded *just* as if someone carrying every cooking pan in the house tripped over at the top of the day stairs and fell the whole way down. God bless us, whatever next? Still, never mind, it's been a dry summer. The weather had to turn in the end. So, now – what have I learned? Of course, just like you, coming here has taught me so much I've sometimes wondered which will explode first, my head or my heart. But even so, even with all I have learned from Father John and Father Theodore, Father Gilbert and all the rest, my first teacher whose words have the deepest roots in my soul, was my mother. And if I had to pick out one thing above all that I learned from her, it has to be that never mind what happens, however much of a pickle you get into, whatever disaster befalls you, there is bound to be at least one thing you can do to improve the situation. Start with that.

"Then, what I want to achieve. Hand on heart, though I do want to be holy and humble and wise and good, the main thing I want to achieve is men well fed. I like to see them looking with interest and hopeful faces as the servers bring their supper in. I like to see them sniff it appreciatively, and reach for the hot bread eagerly, and spread the butter on quick so it melts in. To have been given the privilege of overseeing this kitchen is all I ever wanted and more. All I want to achieve is to be worthy of that responsibility, and feed our brothers well, so they feel contented and satisfied and cheerful. Food comforts us, and strengthens us. There's even food in the heart of our faith at the Eucharist. You see? Jesus knew.

"What my life is about? So, whatever I'd *like* my life to be about, I can tell you what it *is* about – easy for you to remember: food, faith and family; in no particular order. That's me in a nutshell. Sounds horrendously trite, I know, but there you go. It's also true. It's who I am.

"And my last words? Ah, this matters to me. Just as my mother was my first teacher, so my first devotion is to Our Lady. I talk to her every day. And if it works out that way, if the grace is given me, such that I know what I'm doing and saying and that my time is drawing near, I'd like the words of the *Ave Maria* to be the last thing I say before I die. It's been my everyday prayer, and I'd like it to be my last.

"So that's it. See? I told you I could be quick! I hope it fits in with what you need – try me again if it doesn't."

He cocks his head to listen to the sound of the falling rain through the open kitchen door. "I think it's easing up a bit. Might be a good moment to make a dash for it, across to Brother Peter in the stable yard. Thank you for everything, Brother; you're so handy and practical, you have no idea – such a marvellous help to us here." With an airy wave and a smile sent back over his shoulder, Brother Conradus heads purposefully off into the dairy.

How does he do it? Cyril asks himself as he takes his leave and wends his way round the cloister, out through the frater, then sprints across the abbey court to the stable yard. *How does he manage to make everyone who comes into contact with him feel like the best friend he ever had? I am so glad I work with that man.*

* * *

Having failed to track down Brother Peter anywhere near the stables, Cyril thinks to go and look for him at the porter's lodge, where he often gravitates for a chat with Brother Martin on those occasions when work is not pressing.

Sure enough, there he is under the shelter from the rain afforded by the lengthy archway of the gatehouse, along with the guest master Father Dominic, Brother Martin the porter, and their almoner Father Gerard.

Martin is standing in the doorway to the porter's lodge, leaning against the frame of the arched door, his arms folded. The almoner is sitting on the bottom step of the almonry threshold, its door being opposite the porter's lodge in the big gatehouse. Brother Peter has led the abbot's chestnut mare through from the stables and tethered her to one of the iron rings set in the wall of the gatehouse so visitors have a temporary tie-up for their horses. She stands quietly, taking her weight off one back foot. A Percheron, a magnificent beast and a draught horse really, she is contentedly enjoying the attention of Brother Peter grooming her while she chews on a twist of hay. Dominic is sitting on the mounting block that stands hard by the door of the porter's lodge.

These men are not idle, they all have to be on hand for visitors and deliveries, and their daily work centres around the entranceway of the gatehouse. Just for now, their chores are done. Two beds are made up in the guest house in case any unexpected pilgrims arrive, the knives and spoons are sanded and oiled and the fire is laid ready in case it's needed. Brother Martin has been ferrying parcels to their destinations – the checker for the most part – and begging favours of tradesmen to take their letters to recipients in the village. Father Gerard has a huge linen sack of clothing lying on its side on the cobbles of the gateway. He's taking out cast-off garments that have been donated for the poor, and is assessing them for cleanliness (he relies on a basic smell test and shaking them for fleas), then sorting and folding them to take up the almonry stairs to the storage loft.

They pause in their conversation to greet Brother Cyril, and Father Dominic volunteers to fetch him a cup of ale from the guest house. As it happens, they were talking among themselves about his book and its questions, and they are all ready to go with their answers, and not surprised to see him. They thought it must be their turn soon. While Dominic gets Cyril's drink, Brother Martin disappears into the porter's lodge to fetch a pen and an ink horn, and a torn sheet of Cormac's paper from Norfolk with writing on the back. He sets them down on the mounting block so Father Dominic can make notes for Brother Cyril as they go. Dominic has many gifts, and writing impressively fast is one of them.

"Sit down, lad," says Father Gerard, patting the space alongside him on the almonry step, which is worn by the passage of poverty's feet since a hundred years. "What's your preference? Will we go man by man or question by question?"

"The latter," says Dominic, giving Brother Cyril his cup of ale and picking up the pen as he settles himself back onto the mounting block. "It's more economical of words, if you think about it. Each man has only one name. Each question has several words."

So they begin with a consideration of what they have learned, and as he listens to them, Cyril enjoys their lively interest in each other's thoughts.

Brother Martin the porter has learned that although it takes a lifetime to get to know someone, and growing acquaintance can always prove you wrong, even so your first impressions of a man are surprisingly often accurate.

Father Gerard, hearing the unhappy histories of those who come begging alms, has learned how very different people are from each other. You give them each the exact same set of circumstances and you get astonishingly different outcomes. The only thing they usually have in common is that they take credit for what's gone well and think any mishap could not possibly have been avoided; it just happened to them. This outlook on life is what brings most of them back again and again, and they think it is merely good fortune and falling on their feet that keeps the brethren of St Alcuins well supplied with the wherewithal to help them out.

Brother Peter says thirty-two years in monastic life have borne out what he came here knowing already – that horses have extraordinary sagacity. They are great judges of character, they can be trusted to take you home if you get lost or fall asleep, and they are loyal and brave. In truth, he sometimes thinks they might elect a horse to be their abbot one day. When he adds, shaking his head to show he was only joking, "Nay—" Father Martin laughs and says he's even starting to talk like a horse. Brother Cyril, listening to this, thinks it might be a bit tricky to identify from it anything he could include in his book.

Father Dominic, who continues to write as he speaks, says he's learned the remarkable power of Benedictine hospitality, working in the guest house. Pilgrims walk through the door tired and careworn and you can see their burdens ease and lift and leave them as they si down by the fire and sup Brother Conradus's excellent pottage, taste the bread from the morning's baking and the butter made fresh and stored cool.

When they come on to consider what they want to achieve, Brothe Cyril is struck by the sly wit and kindly teasing that flies between thes men, who look so dignified when he normally sees them in chapel. Bu he notices their banter is not hurtful or mean, and eventually Fathe Dominic says, "Right then, lads, what do you want me to set down fo Brother Cyril's book? Unless he has a section planned out for foolis chatter. For myself, working here with guests, what I'm always strivin to achieve – and it's harder than I thought – is to be friendly withou being too familiar, remembering to keep myself in recollection, t be a kindly host but not drawn in to worldly conversation." Cyri drinking his ale, watches how carefully they listen to him, is intrigue by how readily they turn from jesting to serious thought – and tha they evidently enjoy it. So often, before he came here, he saw earne sincerity mistaken for long-faced pretentiousness and mocked. In th place it is safe to let down your guard, to say what you really mea Another thing he notices is that they don't interrupt one another. The let a man finish what he has to say – and, crucially, he *does*; they are not garrulous.

Brother Martin says he's very conscious of being the first brother any visitors meet. He notes drily that many feet find their way here – the folk who walk through that gate do vary. His daily aspiration is to treat each and every one as though they mattered; to extend to each the welcome his heart knows they would always find in Christ, who loves them – all of them – "And by 'eck," he adds, "some of those who walk through this gateway have a ripeness in language matched only by their fragrance."

The almoner says something he now aspires to, that he used not to bother with too much, is keeping the store tidy. With a wry smile he admits that it was during the time Father William was working in the checker – "We all thought he'd be our cellarer, back then," he says in an aside to Cyril – that William had made some choice observations to him about the disorderly state of the store. "Very direct, he was, but I could see his point. He said you might as well not have something if you don't know where to find it or what size it is or can't put your hand on the other half of a pair of shoes or didn't bother to write down that you already gave that heavy coat away last Wednesday. He said my untidiness did the poor out of gifts meant for them, not for us, and further was a disservice to the benefactors who donated it all. And it looked a mess. Yes. As you can tell, it stuck in my mind. But you know, he also set about sorting it all out for me himself. Ever since then I've done my best to follow his example. I try to keep a neat and tidy store, and a full record of what's come in and gone out, with sizes and colours and everything else to help me identify a good match for what anyone in need is hoping to find. It sounds mundane, I know – banal even – but he made me see it matters."

Cyril is intrigued to see the respect with which these words are received. No one says anything rude about William behind his back. No one makes a joke out of Father Gerard's confession of his inadequacy and his efforts to do better – nor do they pretend it doesn't matter or it wasn't so. They just receive it.

Brother Peter says he likewise has no lofty aspirations, but sees the service of Christ in his day-to-day responsibilities – to keep watch over the well-being of the beasts, seeing to it that they are contented and clean, exercised and correctly fed. Horses, he says, can be temperamental as much as men are. They need understanding, you have to know them personally. He says he sometimes thinks he's a kind of Horse Abbot, with his own flock to tend. And he laughs and adds there's a good deal of muck to move with both pitchfork and shovel, every day, and that keeps him from getting too high an opinion of himself. "And all I want to achieve," he says, "is to do it well. So when Father Abbot or Father Prior needs to go riding out, their beasts are all fettled up and ready to go, free of disease and properly shod and in peak condition."

When they move on to what their life is all about, they agree that because they all work here by the gatehouse, and all of them have to do with the abbey's work of hospitality, different aspects of that are always at the forefront of their minds. They talk about it, back and forth, for a few minutes, then Father Dominic says, "All right lads, pick one word each, then. What's your life about? I'd guess welcome and the hospitality of Christ are the heart of it for us all, but mine, in the guest house, is about kindness above all."

"Availability," says the porter, "because how would people feel if they came in through the postern door there, and couldn't find anyone to help them?"

"Readiness," says the almoner. "That's something else Father William said to me – that you're no use if you can't anticipate. There's no point in starting to plant when the famine is now. No use, when people come in January, telling them you'll probably have got some shawls together come May Day. You have to think ahead, to help people in need."

Brother Peter ponders for a moment, and then he says, "Reliability. When you're responsible for living creatures, well, they completely depend on you. You mustn't forget – their food, their water, to let them out and fetch them in. It's essential."

They all agree that their last words are of little importance to them, that if they are faithful in their daily life they can meet their maker in confidence. "Even so?" Brother Cyril presses, shyly.

"Well, just to give thee something for thy book, really," says Brother Peter, "Maybe I'd like to end my life with the hymn we close the day with, at Compline – *Te lucis ante terminum* – and if I'm past singing, which seems likely, I'd be glad to have someone sing it for me."

Father Dominic says one of the most beautiful deaths he can remember was Abbot Gregory of the Resurrection, who had just finished giving the sacred host of the Eucharist to all the community when he felt a little unwell. "Father Chad, who had been assisting with the chalice, stepped forward to finish the final prayers and blessing, while Father Gregory sat down quietly in the bishop's chair at the side of the sanctuary. And then he fell asleep. They let him sleep on peacefully because he was old. As they were singing the recessional hymn, Abbot Gregory went home to his rest. They said he had a smile on his face. So his last words to us – to each one of us," says Father Dominic, "were, 'The Body of Christ.'" I don't know if I'd dare to reach out to take that for myself as well, but I know it would make me happy."

There's a pause when he finishes speaking, that feels tender and reverent. Then Brother Martin, hearing sploshing feet and a gabble of voices approaching outside the gate, steps forward from the door of his lodge into the cobbled way of the gatehouse. As he passes through to open the postern door, he says to Cyril, "I'm often last up, since I'm the man who locks the door. I think it's more than likely the last thing anyone will hear me say is, 'See you in the morning.' Nothing wrong with that, eh, lad? Thanks for what you're doing."

Father Gerard, resting a hand on the almonry door frame to help get himself on to his feet, says quietly to Cyril, "Aye, thank you indeed. What a grand idea! It'll be something every man in this house wants to read, and you can't say that of many books. I think I'd like my last words on this Earth to be the Jesus Prayer – 'Lord Jesus Christ, Son of the living God, have mercy on me, a sinner.' Of course, I might be very short of breath in such a pass, in which case I'm happy to settle just for the second half of it, 'Have mercy on me, a sinner.' The Lord knows me well. He'll know it's addressed to him."

As a novice, Brother Cyril knows he should leave the reception of guests to the brothers in full profession, and make himself scarce when visitors come. So as Brother Martin looks through the postern door and then comes back in to open the gate, seeing quite a party of people walking his way, Cyril takes his ale mug back to the guest house and goes on his way.

There is just time, he hopes, if he's quick, for something he's been meaning to do. He pulls up the hood of his cowl, ducks his head and runs across the court through the rain, going through the church to the cloister, along the north range then hastening through the kitchen gardens to the infirmary, where he pushes back his hood, shakes off as much of the wet as has not soaked in, and goes to find Brother Michael, whom he runs to earth in the dispensary. He politely asks permission to visit Brother Felix. The infirmarian looks surprised and pleased. "Aye, of course," he says. "Nice of you to come over. It's raining cats and dogs out there! Hang on a minute, I'll check."

Today, Brother Felix is willing to see someone, which Michael regards as progress. He takes Brother Cyril along the passage, gloomy on this lowering day, to show him Felix's room. He leaves him at the door. Knocking to announce his presence even though Felix knows, Cyril steps in to the simple, homely room with a fire on the hearth and a lantern burning in the corner. It feels both safe and welcoming in here.

The encounter is short; Cyril is shy of intruding on someone he doesn't really know, who isn't well, and Felix looks tired as he moves very cautiously into a sitting position on the edge of his bed to greet him. He indicates the chair for Cyril to sit down. The novice asks how he is, and Felix says he's doing well, thank you. Felix asks if his notes for Cyril's book were at all what he wanted, and Cyril expresses his appreciation and says it was just right, and so helpful to have it written down – and he comments on how he admired Brother Felix's script, beautifully balanced and very easy to read. Brother Felix murmurs his gratitude for the kindness.

There follows a silence. Brother Felix, sitting on his bed, tense, his weight taken by his hands gripping the edge of the mattress, looks exhausted, Cyril thinks. He wonders if he should just go or begin to chat about what he's been doing. Felix bends his head. Cyril dithers, starting to feel desperate, and then is rescued by the sonorous ring of the bell calling the community to None. He is massively grateful this means he can get up and apologise for having to go.

Felix smiles at him, sort of. "Thank you for coming," he says.

Cyril hesitates, then: "You asked me to pray for you," he says, "in your note. I want you to know, I do – I am doing, every day. I think about you a lot, actually."

This brings a shine of genuine gratitude to Felix's eyes. "Yes, Christopher said you asked him to tell me," he says quietly. "Thank you. Thank you so much. That means more than you might think." He looks at him. "Don't be late on my account," he says. Cyril smiles a farewell, and leaves him in the peace he so clearly needs at the present time.

Chapter Eight

"I've learned," says Brother Mark the beekeeper, in his soft, low voice, "as you might expect, about life in community – how to do it, you know. Some of it I've learned from monks, some from bees, and some from trees. Also birds. They are very good at community. Birds have a gift of watching and communicating. Birds, like bees, gather knowledge and pass on the story. Tell me the next question, lad. What I want to achieve? Thank you.

"One thing only: to play my part. It's important in this life not to go beyond what you should be. Know your boundaries, know your gifts have the measure of your contribution. What you are, what you can do – bring that. The rest is someone else's gift; and leave something for God to do. This is contentment and humility. And your next question Ah. What my life is about.

"This came to me from watching the bees. Their life, and our life in the abbey, is about working together for good.

"Personal ambition, trying to get ahead, self-aggrandisement – thes are very destructive. It takes twelve bees working their whole life lon to make one spoonful of honey. It takes a whole hive to make enoug pots of it for our medicine and our food, to make our candles with the beautiful light. In the human race, just as with the bees, we do we when we travel together. Us, in our daily lives, we've to do as the bee do – chant the psalms, find the nourishment, make the incense and th medicine, tell the story, show the way. If I live with an eye to the need and well-being of all of us, then I am cared for too. If I think and serve and work for only me, then in the end even I will be lost. Bees show us the meaning of a life of service, of all things working together for good. It is as the apostle said, the way we love God."

"Oh," says Cyril. "Is that what he meant? I thought 'all things work together for good for those what love God' meant that things turn out well for us if we are faithful."

"Aye," the old monk smiles at Brother Cyril, nodding in affirmation. "Aye, that's what it means. It's the same thing, d'you see? We are one of the things working together for good. The love, the work, the holiness – it all works together in God; we only have to find our part to play. Do you understand me? Yes? Didn't you have a fourth question, lad? Ah, that was it. My last words.

"Not everyone knows when their time to die is coming, but many men do if they are present to their life and not scattered and dispersed into many distractions – like Mary, you know, instead of Martha; quietly focused, paying attention. I'll wager she knew when her time to die was drawing near. If I am present enough to see it, and God grant I may be, then for one last time before I go to my cell and lie down quietly, I would like to walk down here to the hives, and tell the bees goodbye. Tell them not to be afraid, to watch for their new master.

"That's the thing, isn't it? Look at our life here – peaceful, loving, quiet. There is nothing to fear when all are working together for good. It's envy, carnality, lust for power and wealth and position, desire to own and accumulate, those are the beginning of sorrows. If each one plays his part in working together for good, in service of the common life, then we do well, then fear dissolves. Then we have a quiet mind and it becomes clear that God loves us. A bee can deliver a mighty sting, Brother, but that's the end of the bee."

Cyril finds, as Brother Conradus told him he would when he mentioned this morning that he'd be seeing Brother Mark in the afternoon, a curiously powerful sense of peace in this old man's presence. Sitting here together on folded sacks to protect against the soaked bark, on the sawn logs left to serve as seats in the secluded nook under the oak trees where they keep the hives, Cyril feels the lifting of the breeze against his skin, smells the freshness of the air and the scent of rain in the wind. He can sense one season giving way to the next. Above him, the green has turned to gold, and the leaves are falling. The ground is carpeted with gold. Nearby he sees a few bees visiting the ivy growing on the wall of the small stone building for the garden tools.

It's quite cold, he thinks. He looks at Brother Mark's hands, folded peacefully in his lap, gnarled and reddened, knotted veins standing out on the backs of them. "Are you getting cold, Brother?" he asks, concerned. This man is very old.

"Well, the year's getting on, isn't it?" says Brother Mark. "The nights are drawing in. But I like it, you know? I love the summer days, the flowers, the blue skies. I love the springtime when the leaves break and the birds have their young – the wonder of the dawn chorus before the sunrise. But I love the autumn, when the leaves turn, and the air is fresh, and the wind lifts. Aye, and the winter too, with frost and fires and starlight, and the moon watching over us and the bark of the vixen in the night. Aye, it's cold – but we'd be worried if it wasn't, wouldn't we?

"Thank you for talking to me, lad. Thank you for taking the time. And thank you for thinking to write this book of yours. It will be, when it's done, a revelation of the common life. I hope it will help us see what it means to live humbly, like a bee; to look after one another."

* * *

If you want to find Father James, he's usually in the robing room. If he's not there, he'll be next door in the scriptorium. He binds books for them, and works on the chased silver clasps and corners, as well as making all the clothing worn by every brother in this abbey. Brother Cyril fervently hopes he'll be in the robing room today. Although he inevitably sees Brother Philip in the novitiate teaching circle every morning, he doesn't want to open this venture he's begun to Philip's further scrutiny and the derision that comes with it. Brother Philip works in the scriptorium, and Cyril thinks he'd do well to steer clear of that place until his book is done. "Please," his heart whispers in prayer as he knocks on the door of the robing room; and he's heartily relieved when Father James opens it – and further relieved when a reconnoitring glance beyond him offers the hope of a workshop otherwise empty of human presence. "I'm not going to belittle what you do by asking if you're busy, Father," Brother Cyril says, "but is it possible to have a conversation with you? About the questions I left with you. May I come in?"

Father James welcomes him in and pulls out a stool where he can sit. "I can work and talk," he says, "so will that be all right for you? I ought to get this finished today, really. I've got quite a heap of things backed up waiting."

Brother Cyril appreciates the ambiance of the robing room. Though it lacks the dust and grit of his father's masonry workshop, there is the same sense of order – materials here, tools there, everything in its right place. And that beautiful statue of Our Lady Queen of Heaven smiling on it all from her corner by the window.

"There's never much time for pleasantries, is there?" says Father James as he moves back to his work bench. "Is it best I just plunge in? Otherwise the bell will be ringing for None and you'll have to come back and do it all over again. Er – oh – that wasn't meant to sound as if I thought you were a nuisance! You're not. Come up for a chat any time you need to, there's usually only me here. I just meant . . . well, you know what I meant. I hope."

He looks up, questioningly, from the sea of woven black wool he's spreading out on the bench. *I like this man*, Cyril thinks, *he's easy to be with*. "I know exactly what you mean," he says in reply. "I'm learning that two minutes is enough and five minutes is a luxury. The obligations of the day do certainly stop the devil finding work for idle hands to do. Did you . . . have you . . .?"

"Thought about your questions? Yes? I have indeed. I've been glad of them. It's a great thing you've done, focusing the minds of the whole community all at the same time together, on these matters we do truly need to address. I can remember the first and last ones, but the middle two I forget and then remember again, so you might have to remind me.

"So straight in, then, what have I learned? I found this really interesting to think about. I'm glad you have the abbot's and novice master's permission to talk with us like this, because otherwise I might have hesitated to be so free in my conversation with someone only just admitted and clothed; but they've said we can, so I will.

"Well then, I have to tell you my biggest struggle in monastic life has been with celibacy. It's no secret that I was quite a lad before I came here and I did like the ladies. For the first few months after I gave all that up, I suppose you might say my appetites were satisfied and abstention had a certain restful novelty about it; but it won't surprise you if I tell you, that wore off. And then came the temptations and the hungers and the extremely assertive physical needs. My novice master, Father Matthew, is dead now so you've never met him, and I very much doubt the man is enshrined by many in beloved memory. Don't write that down, will you? That would be unkind. It's true though. I didn't talk to him about these particular struggles, but I know from what others said he was of the 'dowse yourself in cold water, get plenty of vigorous exercise and make use of the prayer of the cross' kind of man. All right as far as it goes, but . . . it makes you a bit . . . I don't know . . . driven, inhuman, something like that. I tried it but it wasn't taking me into anything happier or holier, just wearing me down.

"It stayed a particular cross to bear until we had something of a e-shuffle and Father Francis was priested and became my confessor. t was Father Francis who first caught my eye and intrigued me, made ne think about monastic life before I sought admittance. When I was till thoroughly mired in fornication and drinking yards of ale and Aay Day frolics and self-obsession, I glimpsed the lightness of peace hat is the air that man breathes, and I wanted it for myself. When he ventually became my confessor, he helped me look at life differently. o this thing I want to say to you that I've learned, I mainly owe to 'ather Francis. But what started as his wise guidance became in the nd my daily practice, so I think it would be fair to say I have *learned* t, even it if would be a bit of a stretch to say I'd mastered it.

"So, Francis – Father Francis – taught me to see our life here in ommunity as essentially a practice of simplicity. A jewel of simplicity s how he put it, cut by a master craftsman into facets so you can turn t in the light and see its purity, its beauty, the fire at its heart.

"He said our vows – our obedience to the abbot, our holy poverty, ur vow of stability, and holy chastity – are all facets of the one gem f simplicity. He said to see them all as turning away from accretions nd accumulations, staying free. He said when we make our vow of bedience we lay at Christ's feet, right there and then, all scheming mbition, all aspiration to status and position, all personal agendas. Ve just lay it down. Most lives are bristling with it, and we say, 'Maybe. ut not me.' We give our consent forever to be not the master but only he man. It's how we give our hearts to Christ – to Jesus – our fealty. aying, I am not my own, but yours.

"Then, Father Francis said our vow of stability is to do with taying free of occupation with seeking novelty, and preventing us rom running away from our problems and leaving a mess behind us or someone else to clear up when we go. If you're stuck in the same ouse with the same gang of ruffians the rest of your life, it certainly oncentrates your mind on resolving differences, on sorting out problems, on making things work. And that's an aspect of simplicit as well. Making sure you straighten things out between you whe there's a disagreement or a grievance. Making sure you fix the buildin and its contents, the gardens, the farm and the beasts that live there everything. If you can't leave it, you have to sort it out. To sort it ou you can't let trouble brew. Accumulation always ends in difficulties broken relationships, disease, decay, all that sort of thing.

"Then he said – look, I'm not expecting you to remember a this, just explaining. It's what I want to say about celibacy I'ı trying to get to – he said our vow of holy poverty is the one with a obvious expression of simplicity; not calling anything our own, n attachments, no hoarding, no avarice, no greed. He said those thing are the principle undoing of human society and they carry the seec of war and oppression and misery. He said holy poverty is all by itse one of the greatest gifts God ever gave to humanity. Not the building not the demesnes, not the embroidered vestments and the precioı library of valuable books and the silver of the altars, not the wisdoı and learning and the skills and the theology – none of those, but tł holy poverty, is the treasure of monastic life. That's what he said. T live in such a way that Christ is all, is the sum total of what you hav the only occupant of your heart.

"And that's when he came to holy chastity. He said that, too, is a expression of simplicity. He said the secret to it is not trying to establis or possess. He said holy chastity is characterised by allowing thing to *flow*. He said, whether your attraction is for men or for wome or both, there will be times when you fall in love. Let it come, let sweeten your life, allow the love but don't step towards establishmeı and possession. Just let it flow. Don't try to make it your own. Aboı the needs of our bodies, what we do in solitude, he said to me – b realistic. Sometimes you do, sometimes you don't. Just don't create a accumulation, whether that is of habit or of obsession. Let it be wh it is, let your hungers, your drives, your longings, your needs, be wh they are. Let the thoughts that arise in your mind pass through in peace; don't invite them in to stay for supper.

"He said, the only hope you will ever have of staying open and tender and vulnerable – as you should be, because Jesus is – is if you allow yourself, the man you are, your manhood, your being, to flow and not to build up, not accumulate. He said, don't wallow in carnality like a pig in mud, and don't let it harden inside you like a stone you pick up to throw at people. Just let it be part of your simplicity. Humbly acknowledge that you are simply human. Let it be what it is, let it flow. And when you do fall in love, with all the pain and the beauty it brings, do so with open hands; don't hold on. Even if you want quite desperately to hold it and keep it for your own, to annexe it to yourself, still, open your hand, open your hand, go on opening your hand to let it flow, to let it go. You can lose the clinging and still let love live. You don't need to *have* someone to care about them. Love needs no specific or particular expression. Let it be friendship, let it be esteem, let it be the knowledge of a dear and special resonance between two hearts. Don't turn aside to make it your lodging.

"He said, love is like the Mountain of Transfiguration. It streams and blazes with glory. But the thing is not to make Simon Peter's mistake of offering to build a tabernacle there to house it in. The Lord didn't even dignify that suggestion with a reply. It was just so obviously stupid and redundant. Francis said to let love blaze in you, let love transfigure you; and then walk back down the mountain to the work you have to do.

"In all fairness, he didn't suggest it would be easy, though I have to say, he sounded as if he knew what he was talking about; but he didn't volunteer any personal information, and I didn't enquire.

"Tell me straight, Cyril, am I talking too much? I've been thinking a lot about this, as you can no doubt tell. I mean, this takes letting it flow to a whole new level, doesn't it? Am I overdoing it? Honestly?"

Brother Cyril laughs at the rueful grin on James's face, as he pauses with the shears in his hand. "I won't remember everything you've told me, not in the sense of writing it down word for word – but what I do write down I'll bring back for you to check, to be sure it's you not me it represents. But, when I started out on this, it was all and only writing a book I had in mind. What I'm discovering is that it's going so much deeper than that. What you've just told me will make a difference to how I live, how I practise. *I* will be the book, if you see what I mean."

Father James nods, satisfied. "What was the next question?" he says. "Oh – no, it's all right, I've remembered. What we want to achieve. I imagine several of us, not just me, will struggle with this one. It's hard to hold it in balance with holy obedience, you see. There's a sense in which we're not meant to be trying to achieve anything, more allowing ourselves to be open and empty, to express rather than achieve. Achievement climbs upward where expression flows downward. In holy obedience we express what *Christ* has achieved, it's *his* kingdom – which already exists in full – that we are allowing to come on Earth as it is in heaven, through the availability of our lives. Open. Clear. Simple. But even so, what we want to achieve is a fair question. I think – this is my least definite answer, because it's the question I feel least sure about – but I think that what I want to achieve is purity of heart. Jesus said the pure of heart are blessed because they will see God, and when I say those words I feel it grip my very viscera, I want it so much. Also, as I explained to you, *im*purity of heart has been a big thing for me, the central struggle of my vocation. Learning to let Christ be my first love, and my last. That's what I want to achieve."

He works on in silence for quite some minutes. Brother Cyril reflects that one of the things *he's* learning here is to allow silence to be. Not to break it. To stay with it. But as he sits in the quietness, his thoughts begin to expand. *Purity of heart*, he thinks. *Didn't someone else say they aspired to that?* He can't remember who it was, now. He makes a mental note to look through the ever-increasing pile of pages in his cell, and see if he can find it. And then it suddenly comes back to him. *Oh! The note from Brother Felix!* It intrigues him that Brother Felix with his controlled, precise manner and tense demeanour, so apparently different from Father James's easy, open friendliness, should share the exact same aspiration – not just similar, the same.

"You asked us what we consider our lives to be about," James says, then. "Going back to what I learned from Father Francis – about simplicity being key – I think it has something to do with that. My father was a silversmith, a superb craftsman, and he taught me as much as he could about both design and its execution. Without exception, elegance and beauty are characterised by balance and simplicity. A lot of it is to do with what you leave out and what you take away. So what remains is the essential. That's what you strive for. That's what beauty is. So I thought, if what I learned is how simplicity is the heart of chastity, and if what I aspire to is purity, then what I think life is about is clarity. When you leave out and take away everything that clutters and obscures, clean the panes of the lantern to let the light shine through, patiently skim away the dross that rises to the surface until the gold is purified. Life – monastic life – is about clarity, I think. It is complex, because all life is complex by its very nature, and a good design is often complex; but it is not complicated. It has what it needs and that is enough. Clarity. I'd like my life to be about that, as a craftsman and as a religious man.

"And then, my last words. By heaven, I bet you're glad they're coming! You must have been thinking I'd go drivelling on for evermore! Brother Cyril, this house, this community, has given me more than I could possibly put into words. My love for this place goes so deep I cannot tell you. I would like my last words to be a blessing upon it, on the house and the community. Before I die, I want to say, "I bless you with the love of the Lord," because that's what I found here, and that's what I hope will continue. There! Will that do? So much for paring things down to the bare essentials! Sorry about that. Have you got what you needed?"

Chapter Nine

Glad of a clear dry day, but mainly concerned he may be late, Brother Cyril hurries along from the kitchen door, past the well and through the vegetable garden to the cobbled path that passes from the cloister opening at the angle of the east and north ranges, looping through the kitchen garden and going on through the apple orchard, all the way round to the infirmary. He had to finish up in the kitchen, washing bowls and ale mugs and scrubbing out cooking pots, after the midday meal, so he's walking very briskly, hoping he's not tardy enough to annoy Father William, the man he's coming to see. The truth is, he feels more than a little scared of this infirmary monk, no matter how much esteem Brother Cedd might feel for him. And as for the infirmarian casually calling him "Will" – he cannot imagine it being in any circumstance conceivable to be on such breezily familiar terms with him.

Father William came to find him at the end of Chapter Mass earlier this morning, and said this would be a good time to talk, when the old men would be dozing in their rooms for the most part, and the housework all done in the morning. Come then, he told Brother Cyril.

"Is . . . is Brother Felix feeling better?" Cyril took the chance to say, and immediately wondered if he'd asked something he shouldn't, because Father William looked at him narrowly, thoughtfully, didn't reply straight away. But then he just said, "Yes. He was glad to see you when you called by the other day. He's doing all right. He needs to rest, s all. Thank you."

As Cyril comes through the orchard now, he can see Father William itting on the bench under the cherry tree in the garden, talking with brother Thomas, the abbot's esquire. There won't be many days left his year when it's practical to do so. The storm two days ago shook a ot of leaves down from the trees, and though today the sun is showing hrough the clouds and the breeze has dried the path and the benches, here's a sense of the year turning. It's nice outside, but quite fresh.

As he walks down the path towards them, Cyril can see at a glance ow comfortable and at ease these two men are together. Brother homas is telling him something, gesticulating, laughing, and Father Villiam looks relaxed, his feet up on a stool, an ale mug in his hand, is head turned towards the esquire as he listens to the tale.

Even though he's in a hurry and worried about being late, Cyril an't help thinking, as he comes through the gap in the low wall, how ovely the infirmary garden is with its rosemary and lavender and age, and the cherry trees with their remaining leaves turning pink nd gold now, from the colder nights. It's a kind of paradise. He thinks f Brother Felix taking the time to reintegrate his body and his soul; it vould surely make you well, just spending time here.

Seeing him come in to the garden, Father William takes his feet ff the stool, brushes off the top of it with his free hand and moves it eady for Brother Cyril to sit on. Brother Thomas has a mug of ale, and here's a third one (for him, presumably) standing there on that table, vhich he sees, as he comes up to them, has a chequered surface – a ovely piece of inlay made for chess. One of his parchment sheets with he questions on it lies on the table, held down with a pebble so the reeze doesn't blow it away.

"Wes hal," he says. "I hope I haven't kept you waiting."

"We were just talking," says Father William, "there's no rush. Sit ourself down – if you're warm enough out here. We can go in by the re if you'd prefer."

"No, no – this is just fine. Thank you for making the time to see m Cyril feels suddenly shy in the company of these older men, both wit such an air of assurance, as if they absolutely belonged here, whe he only might. They look at him, Brother Thomas with comfortab friendliness, and the infirmary brother with that particular expressic he has, reminding Cyril of a cat or a fox when something has caug its attention.

"I can see you have my questions," he continues bravely, addressir the remark to Father William. "Will you mind talking about the even though someone else is here?"

He hopes this doesn't sound presumptuous – who is he to te monks in full profession what they should do? – and wonders wh what he said makes Brother Thomas smile down into his ale; and the Father William says, "Nay, that's all right. Brother Thomas – well he's seen me at my worst, and held me when I was at my lowest eb and saved my life. I don't think there's much about me left to surpri him. I can't upset him or disgust him more than I already have." An Brother Thomas just chuckles and says, "Aye, too right. Go ahead. won't butt in. That's your ale, Brother Cyril, by the way."

"So... did you have a chance to give some thought to my questions Brother Cyril asks, somewhat disconcerted by these enigmatic word and not sure what to say other than what he came for. "Thank you," h adds, with a quick smile to Brother Thomas, and has a little drink the ale since they've taken the trouble to get it for him.

"Yes," says Father William, holding his gaze for the moment wit those unnerving eyes. "I did give them some thought. I'll answ your questions, but I also have some of my own if you feel incline to indulge me. What I really wanted to know is why you took off o this endeavour. I'd have guessed you had enough on your plate alrea with novitiate studies and such. Is that not so? Or are you one of tho for whom the world of books is meat and drink?"

He's slightly squinting against the rays of the afternoon sun, brief lifts his hand to his eyes but then shifts the angle of his position instead to benefit from the tree's shadow, which has moved round since he sat down. Even so, Cyril feels absolutely caught in the focus of his unwavering attention. Making up an airy fabrication about having always set his sights on being a writer, or wanting to tell the story of this lovely community, evaporates under the directed intensity of this very strange man's gaze. Quite unintentionally, with no exercise of his will that he can identify, Brother Cyril finds himself simply telling the truth about what happened – about Brother Philip and Cyril the Squirrel on the eve of his naming, and how it robbed it of its joy.

As he gives his explanation he feels anxious lest it sound pathetic and self-piteous. He thinks of Brother Felix, and how much more serious his problems are. He braces himself for laughter, or scorn. Frankly, he imagines he must sound very immature and self-absorbed. The two men just listen quietly; Brother Thomas takes a swig of his ale. Father William sits without moving, absolutely still, looking at him, paying careful attention. The silence continues even when his story trails off into the nothing it suddenly seems. "I'm sorry," says Cyril, lamely. "It seems such a small-minded, petty concern."

"Squirrels," says Father William, in a thoughtful, musing tone, letting his gaze drift toward the trees. "Squirrels are really interesting animals. Brother, have you ever stopped to take a proper look at a squirrel?" His eyes return to Cyril again, in enquiry.

"Well . . . er . . . yes . . . although, er . . . no, not really closely, I suppose. What do you mean?"

"A squirrel," Father William says, "I imagine you are thinking, is some scanty little creature of no consequence. The comparison is demeaning, isn't it? It's meant to make you feel silly and small."

He still looks at Brother Cyril questioningly, his eyebrows raised, and Cyril just nods. Yes. Exactly.

"We have squirrels come down for the scraps we put out for the birds," Father William continues. "They're very resourceful. Mostly you see the arch of their back as they nibble a chunk of bread, or whatever they've scavenged. And sometimes the sun lights up the hair of their magnificent tails – and yes, it's the colour of flame, same as your hair is. Well observed, Brother Philip. What sharp eyes, what sharp wit.

"But sometimes – not so very often, when a squirrel stretches out and up to reach something, you have the unusual and somewhat arresting opportunity to see the front of the squirrel – the belly side of it. The anatomy of a mature male squirrel, good brother, includes much to rejoice in. A squirrel has a lot to be proud of, tucked down there out of sight; possibly more than the asinine half-wit who mocks it. But perhaps he's never noticed nor thought about it. Perhaps neither his wit nor his eyes are as sharp as he thinks. Or maybe it's true what they say and it really does interfere with your vision."

Brother Thomas says nothing, just grins into his ale. Father William gives one cool, sardonic look at Brother Cyril, raises his drink like someone proposing a toast and says, "God bless Brother Philip. Perhaps he's more right than he intended. Maybe there's more to you than there is to him. Perhaps there's something he lacks that he thinks he's got to make up for." He takes a leisurely drink from his cup, then leans forward to pick up the little sheet of parchment weighted down with a stone on the table. "Now, what did you want to know? What have I learned? And what would I like to achieve? You're not aiming low with this thing, are you?

"So, here we are, your first question. What have I learned? I'm glad Brother Thomas is listening; it stops me trying to wriggle out of this with something glib. He knows me too well. By heaven, Cyril, couldn't you have thrown in something easy to get us going? I . . . I . . . Look, I have given all this plenty of thought, I'm not just casting round for an idea; I just find it hard to talk about it." He stops and throws a glance at Brother Thomas, who is sitting quietly watching him and listening to him. Cyril sees what a bond of understanding there is between these two men.

"You asked me once to teach you how to love," the esquire suggests, and Cyril is intrigued by the gentleness of his tone. It's how you would speak to someone you care about, and know very well.

"Aye. I haven't forgotten," says Father William, and Cyril catches the vulnerability in his voice. "And you did. You certainly did. You and our abbot and his sister and the Lord Christ, between you you've done a grand job. It's been . . . devastating. But that's no good for his book, is it? Doesn't every man in Christendom come here to learn to love? To anyone unfamiliar with the history between you and me, it would either sound like a platitude or as though we'd been up to something we shouldn't. I think, Brother Cyril, it would be fair to say that what I've learned here is the diametric opposite of what I learned everywhere else – not a concept, I mean, but something I've learned to *do*. I'd say an art or a skill, but it's not, it's more than that. I . . . I've learned to let people in, to let them see who I am. That's hard for me to say and even harder to do, for all it doesn't sound like much when it's put into words. There's been so damned much pain, you see; I've been protecting it since forever. And our abbot started it off, uncovering what presented to find what was underneath, so he could make a start on cleaning and healing the wounds. He's dug about inside my soul without mercy at times, Father John. Nay, I suppose that's not fair, he's all mercy – but he's certainly gone in deep. Instead of fending him off, I had to be able to let him in. I didn't know how; I'd only learned how to be guarded and well defended. To let people in, to show them who I am, then; yes, that's what I've learned in this community."

He looks up at Cyril, who has the oddest sense of catching sight, for a moment, of the whole world in his eyes. Then he looks down again at the parchment in his hands. "I see you've been economical with this parchment," he says. "You haven't been wasteful. If you'd taken a whole sheet for each one of us, that would have been a lot. Well done. And we can keep them, for a reminder of what we should ask ourselves anyway, from time to time. Why am I here? What am doing? I dearly wish I knew. So then, next you want me to think abou what I'd like to achieve.

"You should know, Brother Cyril, that my principal reputation, anc it's been well deserved, has been for cruelty. Heartlessness. Passin on, perhaps, what was meted out to me, though there's no excuse fo that, is there? Ever. And what I want to achieve, really, is just for tha to stop. I . . . I'd like for people to know they can trust me. The sam as I've learned to let people in, I'd like to think that if *they* let *me* i there wouldn't be absolute bloody carnage within five minutes. I hop I won't ever be someone who can be duped or manipulated – I don' want to be pushed around, I'd still like to be able to stand my grounc and defend what I need to. Stand up for myself. And for the peopl I care about. But I'd like at least the *capacity* for gentleness, so tha a man could know he'd be safe with me. An animal, too. Anythin that can suffer. Gentleness – used deliberately and judiciously. That' what I'd like to achieve. To stop dishing up hurt and become a plac of gentleness. That.

"Well, now then – question three. What would you like your lif to be about? Hmm. D'you mean what would I like to be known for Isn't that the same question as the one before? What am I known for Tom?"

At this, the abbot's esquire smiles. "Apart from caustic remarks anc withering scorn?" he says. "And the capacity for reducing strong me to tears?"

"Oh, thank you," says William, fixing the esquire with a look o shrivelling disdain. "Are you sure you want to spend your whole life i this community, Brother Cyril?"

Cyril feels increasingly out of his depth with this man, but h plucks up courage to say, timidly, "I think, maybe what someone i known for might not be the same as what his life is really about – t the man, I mean. What he's known for might just be in the minds o other people. Like for Brother Philip, what I'm known for, or known as anyway, is being Cyril the Squirrel; but I'm hoping that won't be, in the end, the whole story of my life."

Father William nods. "Aye," he says, in a different, thoughtful tone. "Aye, I can see what you mean." He looks across the garden, thinking. Brother Thomas says nothing more. Cyril waits. Then Father William says, "I imagine you've heard very little about me, other than what I've told you today; but you should know, in the course of my life I've made some bad decisions, a lot of enemies, and some stupid mistakes. Anyone who knows me can testify to the truth of that. But in that same life, I've also been healed by kindness and redeemed by grace. Not *because* of what I am but in spite of it, I have been loved. Which has saved my life in the most literal and physical sense on more than one occasion.

"When I was a lad, Brother Cyril, it's no exaggeration to say I was born into hell. I was beaten and kicked and spat on and abused and reviled, without respite or escape. I grew into the kind of man who lived with a knife in each hand and his back to the wall – figuratively speaking – ready to defend myself and give as good as I got. But what I've tried to struggle through to – often inadvisedly, I have to confess, I usually haven't done it the right way – is to look at the hell they made and say, very well then, this ends with me. I've wanted to be better than the things that were done to me. I've wanted to break the cycle. When I got to know Jesus properly, for myself, I came to realise that he was doing what I was struggling to put in place; it's the miracle of the cross. He takes all the ugliness and cruelty and violence, all the humiliation and shame, and he says, all right then – it ends here, it ends with me. That's what I'd like my life to be about in the end, Brother. I'm sure I'll get most of it wrong because I usually do, but that's what I want it to be.

"How are you going to remember all this? Let me know if you need me to write something down. What else have you got? What would I like my last words to be? Lord have mercy, what are you trying to do to us? This goes a bit deep, doesn't it? And I suppose you're hoping for something honest. Well, then, I've loved the brothers of this house, and they've been so good to me." He looks at Cyril. "They are *right here*," he says, making a fist of his hand and beating it against his heart. "Right here. But I think, to be truthful, I'd prefer to die alone. When it's time for me to go, I'd like it to be private, and quiet, unremarkable and peaceful, like going to sleep. And the last words I say on this Earth, I'd like to say to Jesus. I'd like to say to him, 'I put my trust in you.'"

As he says this, Cyril feels a sudden lurch at the core of his being, as if someone literally took his breath away.

Then, walking rapidly across the grass to them comes Brother Christopher. "I'm ever so sorry to interrupt, but could you come and help me a moment, Father William? I've left Father Paul on his own and – could you just come?"

With a smile and a nod to Cyril combining welcome with apology, Christopher turns and strides back in the direction of the open door. Father William sets down his ale mug, weighs down the sheet of questions under the pebble on the table top again, and stands up to go.

"That sounds rather urgent," he says. "Look, don't lose too much sleep over Brother Philip, will you? Our abbot assures us it's not necessary to eradicate parasites completely. Within limits, he says even worms can be useful. Thank you for your questions, Brother – which, I should tell you, batted away my defences as if they were merely bothersome flies, and walked straight into my heart. God bless you. See you in church."

"I don't believe," says Brother Cyril, slowly, staring after William as he walks away, "that I've ever met anyone quite like that."

Brother Thomas laughs. "I think you just spoke for all of us," he says.

Chapter Ten

When Brother Cyril arrived at St Alcuins Abbey, Brother Ignatius showed him round the claustral buildings, including the pottery on the eastern side of the abbey near the river – you might pass it if you follow the track right round behind the abbot's house, along by the storerooms and up towards the farm. But you might not even notice it if you leave the cloister from the angle of the east and north ranges, passing the chapter house and taking the way through the orchards and kitchen gardens to get to the farm. The infirmary lies to the north-east of the main buildings, and the pottery to the south-east.

Until today, Brother Cyril has had no reason to go back to the pottery. His work is mainly in the kitchens, once his morning studies are done, and he also helps Brother Richard, the fraterer, with the laundry on a Tuesday, and Brother Peter with the horses when he's asked to. His work in the kitchen has taken him to the checker sometimes and occasionally across to the infirmary – not the guest house until he's taken at least his simple vows – but nothing has ever cropped up to take him across to the pottery. That's where he's going now, to see Brother Thaddeus who makes all their bowls and plates and cups and jugs, everything except the pewter cups they have in the infirmary where so many pottery ones got broken. He's also hoping to see Brother Robert, Brother Thaddeus's assistant. He asked Brother Ignatius to point Brother Thaddeus out for him, so he doesn't get them muddled up, and approached Brother Thaddeus to request a time to see him when the midday meal is done.

Walking along the distinctly informal path from the kitchen garden to the pottery – nothing more than stones set here and there into the ground for when it gets muddy – he sees the makings of a kiln being built for firing near the stone workshop. Standing in the doorway, a quick glance round shows him all the usual things. There's the work bench with a variety of rolling pins and knives, ribs and sticks and combs; also moulds for slab-pots, which they use for kitchenware, though they make plates for the frater on the wheel. There are the vats with clay soaking, and buckets of sand of various textures. There's a fairly filthy towel on a nail in the wall. There's a stone sink, with a bound bucket for water underneath it. There's a shelf with some finished pieces, mostly in the green or yellow glazes Brother Cyril is used to seeing, on the usual pinkish clay base. There are three wheels, a low turntable kind, a stick wheel – the stick to turn it is laid across it ready for use – and a double kick wheel. A bucket of water stands hard by the double wheel, which has evidently been in recent use.

"Have you a preference," Brother Cyril asks Brother Thaddeus, "for one wheel or the other?"

"Oh, aye," says Brother Thaddeus, "I'm a lot less keen on the stick wheel because of all the endless bending and stooping to form the clay once it's going. Makes my back ache. There's a lot to be said for being able to sit down to work, in my opinion. We can get it going at a good speed though, so I use it often enough – just not for too long a stretch all at one go. My favourite's the double wheel – the kick wheel. But Robert often works with the turntable wheel, he's happy working low down. Come and sit outside on the bench, lad – you can't sit on anything in here without walking out looking like you'd rolled in mud. Robert'll be along in a minute, he only went across to fetch some water from the well." As they go out of the workshop together, Thaddeus asks him, "Can you remember your questions, or will I go back in and look for them? It's not that I've paid them no heed, just that I'd forget my own name if I didn't have Brother Robert to remind me of it every passing minute."

The bench outside is a long beam supported by two stones that must once have been left over from building the workshop. It has no back, but is placed only just in front of the building, so you can lean against the wall if you want to. Brother Cyril is forming the impression of an enterprise where men are used to doing their best with very little money spent on them, the provisions being adequate for purpose but certainly not sophisticated. The potters have what they need, and nothing more. Thaddeus, still wearing his capacious wrap-around apron, his habit kilted up underneath so his bare feet are free for the wheel and the skirts of his habit don't get caked in clay, indicates the bench to Brother Cyril in a gesture of hospitality. Like everyone else Cyril has met here, he entirely lacks pretension; he is comfortable with the simplicity of his surroundings.

Brother Robert comes walking towards them holding steady two buckets of water suspended from a wooden yoke on his shoulders. "Two is heavy," comments Brother Thaddeus, "but it saves a second trip."

They watch Brother Robert set down his burden with care not to spill the precious water. "Sorry to keep you," he says, and steps into the workshop to fetch an empty bucket and a sack. He inverts the bucket to sit on, and folds the sack to go on top of it as padding.

"Right," says Brother Thaddeus, "we're all yours. Go on, then, lad – first question?"

"It was what you've learned," says Brother Cyril, "and that could be anywhere, but as this is a book about the community, I mainly had my mind on what you might have learned here."

He looks at first Thaddeus and then Robert, as they think this over. Thaddeus is about the same age as the abbot's esquire, he thinks, heavy-set but not corpulent, just brawny. He has big hands with stubby fingers; evidently he's washed them, but there's still plenty of clay around his fingernails and in all the folds and creases of his skin. His hair, once brown, is greying now, untidy around his tonsure. His face is ruddy and weathered by sun and wind; his brown eyes are kind. Robert, who Cyril assesses as not much older than himself – in his early twenties, perhaps – is likewise a strapping lad, with a similarly peaceable and unpretentious air. They remind him, somehow, of a team of oxen – strong, and capable, and calm.

"I'll go first then, will I, Robert?" says Brother Thaddeus. Cyril has the feeling he is something of a father figure to the younger man. Brother Robert nods, and waits with interest to hear what his mentor has to say.

"A thing I learned early on in my time here, that's stood me in good stead ever since," says Brother Thaddeus, "I just picked up from watching and listening, from noticing what people said and did – but equally as much from what they didn't do and say, that they could have but they thought better of it. We have some good men here, Brother Cyril. Don't we, Robert?" His assistant nods in very definite assent, and Thaddeus's face softens into a smile.

"Each of us has a different role to play, but all of us live in community. There's silence, aye indeed, and solitude in our cells, but as you'll discover for yourself, you really do need to be able to get on well with other people, if you want to live here. It's a godly place, I hope; I'm quite sure it's very human. And what I noticed is something we all have in common, whether it's wholesome or not I couldn't say, but it's true, is that every man here has a deep need to feel good about himself – you know? To feel he's doing all right, he's appreciated, he's wanted. And I've come to see that just with a few encouraging words, a bit of appreciation, remembering to say 'thank you' and 'well done' and 'that's just grand', you can help anyone you meet fill that deep need he has, to feel good about himself. People, life, all of it, it's just simple really – and kindness is the key that unlocks it all. Anyone can do it, everyone appreciates it. It's like being able to work miracles, without having to be a martyr or a saint. But, how about you, Robert? What have you learned?"

Despite the gentleness with which the question is asked, Cyril sees the faint gleam of alarm in Robert's eyes. He suspects that getting things right has not been this young man's forte.

"When I think about what I've learned," says Brother Robert, "it feels like looking in to a box of bits and pieces, everything muddled in together. I'm not too sure what to pick out. But here's one thing I've learned. People can be kind to you – give you things, make a place for you, be nice to you – and it doesn't usually make you feel great. You just know they're making an effort because they're nice people and they have to. Or you can be kind to them, and that doesn't feel great either, because you have nothing to offer that they want, and it was someone else's opinion they were interested in. They say it's more blessed to give than to receive; well, it might be more virtuous or noble or something, but in my opinion neither giving nor receiving is what makes you feel good. It's what you share. What you do together. Working together, eating together, being allowed to belong. You don't want to be thrown a crust by someone who walks away – nobody does. But if someone breaks their crust in half and sits down to eat it with you, well, you get half as much bread but twice as much happiness. And even something you didn't really want, maybe hard work like digging or cleaning up, if you share it and do it together it completely changes. It's being left alone to do it all by yourself, because no one else wants the job or wants your company, that makes it feel bad. It's kind of like sunlight, sharing is; it makes it a nice day."

"That's truth," says Brother Thaddeus respectfully. "That's wisdom, that is." When he sees how pleased Brother Robert looks at this approval, Cyril thinks he's just seen Brother Thaddeus's miracle-working in action. "Thank you," he says. "That's so good. D'you remember my next question? What you want to achieve."

Brother Thaddeus frowns up at the sky. "Well," he says, "there's something I do as a kind of habit, but I plan to go on doing it every day, so maybe it can count as something I want to achieve. When I get up in the morning, it's with the intention of finding something special in the day. Maybe something wise, or beautiful, something that speaks right into my heart. It can be a part of nature, like the sunrise or raindrops on a spider's web, or else something Father John says in chapter that takes me by surprise and makes me see life differently. It can be a piece of music the lads have practised for Mass – and when it's that, then most often it's my favourite pieces that really lift my soul, more than something I've never heard before. It could even be the glossy marvel of a conker fallen from a horse chestnut tree – i can be anything. But I get up in the morning, and in my own private devotions I ask the Lord Christ, 'What'll it be today, Master? What will I find that's special?' There's always something. And – I'm not sure I'm answering properly, this isn't an achievement is it? But I just want to go on doing that."

Brother Robert, though he has been listening with all due respec and attention, is obviously bursting to say something. "How abou you, Brother Robert?" Cyril prompts.

"Easy," says Robert. "I want to persuade Father Abbot to let u make some red-glazed pots, like the ones they make in Scarborough

Brother Thaddeus laughs. "Eh – thank you, lad – he wants to d that for me, Brother Cyril. I've set my heart on making some red pots but Father says no. The glaze is poisonous, he says. But still . . . I'd lov to have a go. Red pots! Imagine! How lovely would that be? Brothe Robert knows it's what I've set my heart on. I'm not sure that's the kin of thing he had in mind though, Robert."

Brother Robert asks Cyril if he's right in thinking the abbot will b reading this book. When Cyril affirms this is indeed the case, he say "Red glaze it is, then. Keep it in."

When Brother Cyril reminds them of the next question, wh they would like their life to be about, Brother Thaddeus says, after moment's thought, "You know, mostly when I hear people talk about life – what it's for, what they want to do with it – what they have in mind is life as the tool or the material, and they are the craftsman. So someone might say, for instance, 'What will you do with the afternoon?' But I have this hunch – well, I might just be lazy, but I hope not – that life is not really like that. Even sitting here, looking around at the grass and the stones, the trees yonder, the weeds growing at the base of the wall, those great clouds sailing by overhead – by 'eck, it's magnificent isn't it? Or if you look at your hand, the joints, the nails, the muscles, the veins, the stretchiness of skin; I mean, isn't that astonishing? So, I've gradually come to think that what we came here for, what life *is* actually about, is just the chance to see it, hear it, touch it, feel it, wonder at it. God's handiwork. God's design. I . . . truly, I think we are here to be amazed. I think that's why he invited us; he wanted to show us what he had made, and see how beautiful it is."

Brother Robert, listening to this, nods in approval. "Like Brother Walafrid's cell," he remarks.

"Oh, glory, yes!" says Brother Thaddeus. "Have you seen Brother Walafrid's cell?" he asks Brother Cyril. "No? Ask him to show you. He won't mind, he'll be pleased."

"I think life is just about doing our best," says Brother Robert. "What else could it be?"

Cyril thinks there is a certain immovable common sense about this. It appeals to him. "Just one thing more, then," he says. "What your last words might be."

"I'd like it to be something edifying," says Brother Thaddeus, "but the truth of the matter is that every brother in this house knows perfectly well I'm as thick as two short planks. Not only would they be astounded if I dropped some pearl of wisdom in my dying moments, but I think the chances of it are surpassing slender. Even if I could come through with it, I doubt it's what anyone would want of me. I think in all honesty, the most useful last words from me would be some instructions written down for any jobs left unfinished. I mean, that's what they'd need to know, don't you think?"

Brother Robert says he hopes he's not going to die for quite a while, although he acknowledges it's true you never know. But he says he hopes when he does go it'll be quietly in his sleep and he'll know nothing about it. To be honest, he knows he shouldn't be, but he's a little bit scared of dying. So, if it works out the way he hopes, then the last words he'll say will be the Office of Compline. And he thinks that might in any case be just right.

Brother Cyril walks away from the pottery feeling slightly confused. He can't work out if what he's heard from these two men is so commonplace and so banal he might as well not have bothered, or if he's just had truth you could live by forever gently entrusted to his hands to immortalise. He supposes it all hinges on whether people actually live by what they say. He feels uncertain about his abbot's response to the longing for red glaze being recorded for posterity in the abbey library. And he wonders what's so unusual about Brother Walafrid's cell.

* * *

Several old men live in the infirmary. Consulting the list Father Theodore has given him, Brother Cyril sees there are five, and thinks it's time he made a start on talking with them, so once None is concluded he walks across to ask if that will be possible. He finds three old men sitting outside, well wrapped in shawls and with rugs tucked over their knees, now the days are getting chilly. He can't find anyone else. Going in to the infirmary building, he eventually hears voices he recognises – Brother Michael's and Father William's – coming from the room of one of the residents. He pauses to listen, but it sounds from what they are saying as though they might be involved in some care procedure, so he doesn't like to disturb them. He heard singing as he was walking past the east end of the abbey church, and he knows Brother Christopher often sings in some of Father Gilbert's more ambitious music at High Mass on Sunday – they'd be practising today, so he could be there. In the end he decides to take the plunge and talk to the old men by himself. He's not sure of their names.

He takes out a stool from the infirmary frater, and sits beside one of the old men, who at least appears to be awake.

"Good day to you, Father," he says politely. "My name is Brother Cyril."

"Eh?" says the monk.

He doesn't want to shout because he's reluctant to distract the infirmarians from their work inside, so he just tries again, enunciating rather more clearly.

"Eh?" says the old monk again. "I can't hear a word you're saying, lad. Shall I ring for Brother Michael?"

Worried, Cyril shakes his head emphatically, places his own hand over the old man's to stop him reaching for the bell, smiles at him, and gets up. He looks at the other two men. One is fast asleep, snoring slightly and dribbling. The other one says, "Is there any way I can be of help, Brother Cyril? My name is Father Clement. Are you the young man who is writing a book?"

Though the aged monk turns his face towards him, Cyril realises he cannot see. He takes his stool to sit beside him. "Thank you so much, Father Clement," he says with relief. "Yes, I am asking every brother for a response to four questions I had, for my book."

"Yes," says Father Clement. "Brother Michael said you would be coming. Would you like to hear my answers? I have them prepared and memorised."

"Er – thank you!" says Cyril, taken aback. "Yes – please do go ahead."

"Something I have learned," says Father Clement, "is that arguments are a complete waste of time. Transformation and insight do not arrive that way. Argument merely entrenches division and fosters resentment. It is example, and only that, by which you can change someone's mind.

"What I would like to achieve, limited though I now am, is helpfulness. You know, if you can help one person rise up from melancholy or shame or feeling lost, you have helped the whole human race take a step forward. Every small thing makes a difference." He smiles. "That's what I tell myself these days, anyhow. I hope it's true. So I try to be as helpful as is still within my power.

"You asked what we would like our lives to be about. Mine used to be about producing beautiful manuscripts in service of Christ. I was proud of what I did. I loved my work. My life now is about learning humility; to accept with patience the will of God, to respond graciously to whatever is required of me, to wait patiently, and to do my best to retain such dignity as I can. All this requires humility, because it is such a long way down from how I used to be. There is no more beautiful Christian virtue than humility. I hope I can prove worthy of shaping my life around it.

"My last words? One passage, that I remember stood out to me from the page when I was writing out a psalter for chapel. It was in Latin, of course, but what it meant was 'Thou wilt show me the path of life. In thy presence is fulness of joy. At thy right hand are pleasures for evermore.' I say it to myself every day. Life has been so difficult in recent years. I will say it one more time, to give me courage. Brother Cyril, thank you so much for taking time to come and see me. May this endeavour of yours be blessed indeed."

He stretches out his hand to find Cyril's, and smiles in his direction. "Thank you," says Brother Cyril. "Thank you so much, Father Clement."

* * *

Brother Cyril goes for a walk with Brother Ignatius after supper, and then straight to Collatio and Compline. He doesn't get back to his cell until it's time to go into silence. He's taking his candle to light from the one in the passage when he makes out that someone has pushed a letter under his door. Intrigued, he puts the candle on its little shelf, picks up the letter and takes it across to read by the light of the flame.

"I gather you got no joy from Br. Paulinus and Fr. Gerald," it says. "Sorry. Come and see them any time, but I took the liberty of shaking them hard until some words fell out of their mouths. On what they've learned, Br. P says never give up; men rely on your example. Fr. G says rest is not time off, it can be highly productive. What they want to achieve? Br. P says, given the pain in his joints, just to be civil is enough sometimes. Fr. G says he gets muddled and forgets; he wants to at least be gracious and not an inconvenience. What life is about? Br. P says it's like wise planting (he was a gardener); it's all about getting the right man in the right conditions and location, then they flourish. Fr. G says it's often a matter of timing: when to be quiet, when to speak, when to act, when to be still. Watch for the *kairos*, he says. Last words? Br. P looked at me as if I was mad and said, the Lord's Prayer obviously. Fr. G said it would be a prayer to be taken into the sacred heart of Jesus. Hope that helps. Sorry we were busy. Fr. W."

Chapter Eleven

Today Brother Cyril has to go to the abbot's house after the midday meal, for a meeting with Father John to discuss his vocation. This will be a regular occurrence as he passes through his novitiate year, but for him it still feels new. Of course, he came to see the abbot when first he asked to be admitted as a postulant to try the life, and he met with him again before he was clothed and tonsured and given his name in religion – but that's only twice. This feels nothing like routine. On both the previous occasions, though he found the abbot to have a kindness and warmth about him that won Cyril's heart, he could not have called it a comfortable experience; the questions Abbot John asked him, and the level of honesty he clearly expected, felt searching indeed. He had walked away knowing he'd been very carefully sifted and examined.

He stands in the cloister for quite some while gathering the resolve he needs to actually knock on the door – which, unusually, is closed. He hopes he's not interrupting anything. Then he lifts his hand and raps firmly with his knuckles against the dark, heavy oak. There is no immediate reply. He wonders what to do, but he is supposed to be here, so he knocks again. Brother Thomas, the abbot's big, burly esquire who was with Father William in the infirmary garden, opens the door. He has a broom in his hand.

"Hello," he says, looking enquiringly at the novice. "Can I help? Father's not here. I think he said he was going across to the infirmary to see Brother Felix." He sees that Brother Cyril isn't carrying anything to drop off, and he doesn't immediately communicate a message, so it seems unlikely he's been sent here on an errand. "Was it something important?" he asks, looking again. Cyril seems somehow disappointed.

"I . . . er . . . he asked me to come and see him," explains Brother Cyril. "Just to talk about my vocation and how I'm getting on. No, I – er – I suppose that isn't really important. It's just what he wanted to do."

"Oh! Strewth!" says the esquire. "I'm so sorry! It must have slipped his mind. Look, why don't you come in? I don't know how long he'll be. Actually, it's lucky either of us is here. I've been spending my afternoons up on the farm helping with the threshing, but I thought I'd better take an hour to tidy up in here. Come on in. I'm only sweeping up and cleaning the hearth. You can sit in the corner and point out the bits I've missed." He opens the door fully and steps back to welcome the novice in. "I'm really sorry," he says, looking again at Cyril's face.

"Something I notice here," says Brother Cyril, coming in to Father John's atelier, and following Brother Thomas to the chair that he pulls back to indicate this is where the novice might like to sit, "is how much everybody – all the time – apologises."

The esquire laughs, "Aye, and now you can see why," he says. "We don't know what we're doing, we aren't where we should be – and that's just the abbot! Sit down, lad. Oh, I tell you what, though, since you're here – why don't I give you my two penn'orth on the subject of those questions you handed out to us in Chapter, that you went through with Father William over in the infirmary? Now's as good a time as any, isn't it? I've given it plenty of thought. Is that— does it make it feel a bit more worthwhile traipsing over here?"

Seeing this immediately sparks interest and enthusiasm, Brother Thomas stands the broom against the wall of the fireplace, and pulls up the other chair that stands near the hearth.

"All right, then" he says. "You'll probably have to prompt me, but I can certainly remember your first question, because it kept me awake half the night. What have I learned?"

Something in Brother Tom wants to take the easy way through this – keep it light, hold it at arm's length with a few jokes. He acknowledges to himself that this is exactly what he might have done if the lad hadn't shown up unexpectedly like this, looking so crestfallen that Abbot John had forgotten all about him. Tom is fully aware that his abbot will be horrified when he realises he's overlooked something that matters deeply to somebody else, as if it had been of little consequence to him, and he can see it will repair it for both of them if he can turn this into an opportunity for something of value and authenticity. So he takes a deep breath and commits to being actually honest.

"I've learned," he says, "to bring myself fully and completely to an encounter. Of course, after spending half an hour with me, you might disagree, but I hope not.

"I mostly learned that from our previous abbot – I was his esquire, too. He had a leg never healed from something that happened to him, and broken hands too. Then he was taken ill, and partly paralysed and lost his speech for a while – and yes, it was every bit as bad as the look on your face suggests. He went through hell, that man, and I don't mind admitting I was frightened to walk through it with him. I avoided him for a while, I'm ashamed to say, after he fell ill, and it was Brother Michael and Father John – who was our infirmarian then – who came and hooked me out of hoping it would all just go away, and made me come back and face it with him.

"Since that time I've had a hero: Simon of Cyrene. He was strong, and he came in from the country. I could identify with that. There was nothing he could do about the crucifixion of Jesus – he didn't understand it and he wasn't prepared for it, and he was a bystander not a volunteer. Something very similar happened to me with my abbot then. I was just on the sidelines. But Brother John (as he was then) and Brother Michael came and roped me in. They made me help, and

I assure you I was most reluctant. That's what happened to Simon of Cyrene, isn't it? 'Come on, lad – you'll do,' they said to him. And they made him carry Jesus's cross because it was too much for Jesus. Being crucified is hell on earth. At least Simon didn't have to go through that. But carrying a cross isn't much fun either, as I discovered.

"Anyway, since that time, Simon of Cyrene always had a special place in my heart, a shrine on the wall or something. It made me see that a man has his own path to walk and his own burden to bear, his own death to face – but sometimes you can walk the *Via Dolorosa* with him, and for a little stretch of the way help him carry his cross.

"And between the despair my abbot fell into and the incontinence that he hated, and that he couldn't walk, but above all that he couldn't speak much at all at first, it offered quite a challenge when it came to communication. That's the thing I learned. I came to see that much of what passes for encounter, and keeps us rolling along in the general way of things, is extremely superficial. Chit-chat and jokes and banal truisms, just words that come out of our mouths to be pleasant and cheerful. It's not without value, of course – I mean, who wants to live in community with men who are morose and silent, or, for that matter, men who want to look deep into your eyes and pierce your soul every passing day? There's a place for a cheery platitude in the daily round. But I tell you, it was no good to him.

"I learned to venture beyond words and hold his hand. I learned to take him into my arms and hold him close when he was terrified and couldn't see a way out of what had become intolerable. I learned to just . . . not go away. To stay with him. Because his own reserves were exhausted.

"But it didn't end there. There was also Father William – from the infirmary. I wouldn't tell you this unless I was sure it would have his blessing, but I think I can say I know him well enough to feel confident he'd say, yes, go ahead. He told you he and I have a history, and I have to confess, Brother Cyril, I used to hate that man. He . . . well, he's a complex individual. He had a miserable, terrifying childhood, and he started monastic life in a fairly savage institution, and all of it made its mark. On the occasion of my first meeting with him, he bullied our abbot – who was, as I said, a man who had to live with a significant level of disability – he bullied him mercilessly. I thought there was no power on Earth or in heaven that would ever induce me to forgive him. The place he came here from burned down – set alight, everyone else hated them too – and he took shelter in this house because no one else would have him. He showed up on our doorstep the exact same time as Father John became our abbot, and I gave both of them a hard time because I cut up rough. I did not want him under our roof, and I took every chance that came my way to make that as plain as I could. I thought it a desecration of our abbot's memory.

"And I had my way. In spite of Father John pleading with the community to take him in, I persuaded them otherwise, and they said no, he couldn't stay. But then everything got turned around when I went into the barn up on the farm and found he'd strung himself up from a beam. Yes."

Cyril's mouth has actually dropped open. "You – tried to kill himself, you mean?"

"Aye, that is indeed what I meant. Anyway, me and Stephen leapt to it and managed to cut him down in time – just – and Stephen legged it down the track to find Father John, leaving me kneeling on the barn floor with William in my arms throwing up. And that's when things started to change. It didn't happen all overnight, not by any means, but I learned to find a way out beyond what mattered to me and how I saw things, to begin to understand his point of view. Getting to know him better made me see, if something goes wrong in community, you can get a circle of blame forming, each man pointing at the next man telling him what he's doing wrong. And it doesn't matter if every single one of them is right, nothing's ever going to change that way, is it? It's only when someone stops and looks at what he can put right in himself that there's even half a chance of anything shifting. I was so lucky that in my case, this one occasion I'd got into a complete bind I couldn't get unstuck, William knelt on the floor in front of me, and gently kissed my feet, and asked me to forgive him. Nothing had materially changed, but somehow it stopped being a problem at that point. The glue that held it all into a dense mass I couldn't work with, just dissolved. And I saw . . . him . . . not a problem, a man. And what you said to me the other day – that you'd never met anyone quite like him – aye, right, me too. I haven't either. He's had a distinctly wild ride in his time with us – he was out four years, he married Father John's sister – and life alongside him is never dull. But, Brother, he's come to be so dear to me, so . . . loved, is all I can say.

"And I wouldn't have looked for any of this, it grew by itself out of the muck and grit of men's suffering. Our Abbot Peregrine, and Father William, both of them, what they went through took them down as low as it's possible to go. There was nothing anyone could do to make it bearable, for either one of them. I'm skipping great chunks of their stories of course, there's more to it than I've told you, but there were times when all I could do for either one of them was just hold them and let them weep. Aye – that's right.

"And then our Father John has had some horrendous things thrown at him, too; things that brought him to his knees, just racked with grief and self-accusation and . . . well, he hasn't had it easy. And the thing I've learned is, when it's like that, there is absolutely nothing you can do, nothing you can say, nothing you can offer, except only one thing – the willingness to be present, to be there with them, to not run away. To say that wasn't my first instinct would be an understatement. But it's the main thing I've learned from my years in monastic life. And *because* of it – just because I stayed, and was with them as they went through their various hells – they lodged in my heart. I came to love them. So . . . that's what I've learned."

He looks at Cyril, nodding. "Aye. That's what I've learned. And frankly, I think that might be the only thing."

The novice can't think of anything to say in reply. Tom grins at him. "I want to say it wasn't as bad as all that, but that would be the cheery evasion I hope I left behind; it *was* that bad. And thank you for listening, and what was your next question? I did read it, I did think about it . . . but . . ."

He lifts his eyebrows in enquiry, and Brother Cyril pulls himsel together to say, "Erm – what would you like to achieve?"

Brother Thomas runs his hand across his head, grimacing uncertainty. "Achieve? I . . . well . . . two things, I guess. I'd like to make sure that, between me and Stephen and Germanus, our monaster buildings are in as good a state of repair as they can possibly be. I'd lik the barns to be filled and the stock to be healthy as well, but there's a certain amount of happenstance to that. But the farm buildings – wel that's diligence, that's keeping on top of it. If the buildings are in goo repair, then everything else you try to do has a better chance, in m opinion. Men don't do so well if they're cold and wet and the beast are sick and the roof leaks. So, while I've my health and strength, that' the first thing. Then the second is, I'd like our abbot to know I've go his back – that when he comes in here tired or dispirited, when thing aren't going as he hoped, he's going to find a friend, someone he ca trust, who will always believe in him, never let him down. I hope I'n a good friend to anyone who needs me, but – our abbot especiall Those two things. Is it allowed to have two? That's what I'd like t achieve."

He looks at Cyril. "I'm worried now that I shouldn't have told yo any of that. Especially about William. It . . . well it was indiscree wasn't it? I mean, for mercy's sake, you know you can't write any c that down, don't you? About how he treated our abbot – it's commo knowledge, but . . . it can't be written down. And the other, abou trying to hang himself, well, our bishop . . . he . . . because Willia was out of monastic life for those years, although he was still a pries still a monk, it made him vulnerable – because he could technically be considered apostate – it took away the protection he had from capital punishment and, as you'll be aware, suicide's a felony . . . he . . . the bishop wanted him both excommunicated and hanged. So . . . we think the bishop's moving to Durham shortly, but . . . oh, God, I should never have told you all this. I don't know what I was thinking. We try – ha! – to be cagey about him. Please don't write it down. William, he once asked me – I think I told you the other day – if I would teach him how to love. And in reply I asked him, then, if he could teach me to think before I speak. He said that would be impossible. He was right, wasn't he?"

"Maybe," says Brother Cyril carefully, "you didn't tell me anything at all about Father William? Maybe you simply told me that what you've learned here is to bring your whole presence to an encounter; to let it be authentic and real, because that's what love asks of us. And what you would like to achieve is to make both the visible building of stone and mortar, and the invisible building held together by love, as sturdy as it's in your power to do. Is that fair? Am I putting words into your mouth?"

He thinks Brother Thomas looks immensely relieved. "Thank you," says the esquire, relaxing. "You've got a wise head on your shoulders – wise beyond your years. Thank you so much."

Brother Cyril smiles at him. Before he embarked on this, he would not have imagined needing to set someone in full profession at their ease, having them confide in him more than they intended to. It's coming as quite a surprise to him. "So," he says, "that's settled, then. Did you have a chance to mull over the next question – what you would like your life to be about?"

Brother Tom looks at him blankly. "Yes, I'm sorry, I'd forgotten that one. The thing is . . . oh dear, this is going to be such a let-down . . . I don't feel really that my life is *about* anything. I just . . . live. What I am, who I am, it's not got enough forethought to be *about* anything. I just arrive at the place where I am, and the time – I'm in this moment and with this person, and that's what it is. There's my vows, of course – I'm vowed to be Christ's man, I've promised. I want to be true to that. want it to be the whole of me. Not just what the vows are, of stability and fidelity and obedience, but something that's all of a piece. So if you were with me you would feel safe, and I could help you be the person you were meant to be, just by being with you. That . . . I think that's what the Lord Christ does for me."

"Might it be fair to say," suggests Brother Cyril tentatively, thinking back to something Father Theodore said to them earlier in the week "that what you've described to me there is the *shalom* of God? To be fully present and fully human and fully alive? To establish yourself so much in wholeness that other people find their way into the wholeness by being with you?"

"Yes," says Tom. "Exactly that. The *shalom* of God. I— thank you."

"I don't know if you remember," Cyril prompts him then, "but the last question was what you'd like your last words on this Earth to be."

"Oh, glory," says Tom. "I should think what I'd be most likely to say is, 'Time to go home, thank the Lord!' No, not really, I'm only joking I don't mean that. Although, from what I saw of Father Peregrine's last year of life, and some of the other men they had in the infirmary then, when it comes to it, that might be exactly what I think. I suspect it was what he would have said, if he hadn't been past speaking. But again, you can't write that down, can you? It's hardly edifying, and this is a book, after all. Perhaps, if we assume that my last words would be spoken to someone who was actually listening, rather than just talking to myself, or praying, then maybe I'd like it to be that the last thing said to anyone with me might be, 'It'll be all right. Don't worry. It'll all be all right in the end. If we . . . if we stick together.' That's what I'd like to leave them with, because that's honestly what I believe is true."

"Yes," says Brother Cyril, softly, as he considers this. "Yes. That sounds . . . that sounds absolutely right."

The latch clatters and the door opens precipitately, making them both jump. Brother Cyril reads in Brother Tom's eyes a fleeting glimpse of sudden panic, and realises he's still acutely anxious about having said too much. But – "Oh, my brother, I'm so sorry! I'm so very sorry!" says their abbot, striding across the room to where they're sitting. Both of them hastily stand, as they're supposed to do, and Cyril sees the kindness and contrition and concern in his abbot's face. *I love this place*, he thinks. *This is where I want to make my life.*

"Please don't worry," he says. "Brother Thomas has been talking to me about my questions, his thoughts for my book. And I'm sure Brother Felix really needed you, where seeing me was something we could easily rearrange."

He smiles, and he sees the abbot relax. It comes to him that most of all, this has been an afternoon for learning about authenticity. *That was so intensely . . . real*, he thinks.

As Brother Cyril takes his leave of them, and Tom closes the door behind him, he turns resolutely to face his abbot. "I'm really sorry, Father," he says. "I think I've been indiscreet. I was thinking on the spot, and I just told him whatever was passing through my mind. If I'm honest, I said far more than I should have done."

His abbot laughs. "Yes, I don't doubt it," he says. "But thank goodness you were here, and you talked to him about something, eh? But when you say you said too much, Tom, what do you mean?"

His esquire looks at him with apprehension. "I told him about the pathway William and I travelled to become friends. And that he was married to Madeleine. And about the animosity the bishop holds towards him."

"Oh," says John, thoughtfully, taking this in. "I see. You . . . yes, you did tell him a lot, didn't you?" He glances at Tom, sees he looks absolutely wretched. "Ah well, never mind. Nothing improves by worrying about it, does it? Let's just hope he stays with us and has the sense to keep things to himself. You did tell him to keep it quiet?"

"Yes, I did. And not to write any of it down. He grasped the importance of that."

His abbot nods. "Don't worry. You did your best with a situation dropped on you. Just let it be what it is. Things will work out. We . . well, God is with us. We have help."

Hastening up the stairs in the direction of his cell, Brother Cyril holds the conversation he's just had vivid in his mind, going over it again, thinking about Brother Thomas and Father William. *This is a healthy place*, he thinks. *Where else have I ever been where they know how to turn enmity into friendship, and how to say sorry so often and so humbly, and really mean it? I don't suppose it's an easy life, but I'm going to stay here.*

Chapter Twelve

After the midday meal, two aged monks make their way into the kitchen. One of them has a quiet word with Brother Conradus. He listens and smiles, picks up two stools and carries them across to the fireside for them, and then goes in search of Brother Cyril who is in the scullery scrubbing the pan they used to cook the fish. If it's just vegetables and legumes and grain, you can let it build up and it only adds to the flavour. Fish matters.

"Brother Fidelis and Brother Prudentius have come to see you," says Conradus, "about your book."

"Er . . . who?" Brother Cyril sometimes wonders if he'll ever get to know everybody properly.

"They work in the garden," says Conradus. "The roses in the cloister garth are Brother Fidelis's life's work, so I'm told. That's why they're so beautiful; because he loves them. Leave that pan, I'll get to it in a minute; and if I don't, I feel sure it'll wait. Let it soak a while. I'll put some vinegar in it."

So Brother Cyril goes through and joins the two old men warming their hands by the kitchen fire. He brings a third stool to sit with him. He thinks their faces are like a story all of its own, the kindness in their bright, perceptive eyes, the weathered skin of their faces etched with deep lines from years of frowning in concentration and sudden smiles.

He discovers that Brother Fidelis has learned to leave things, to set down his tools and turn to prayer when it's required of him. It was a hard lesson at first, but he learned to find its rhythm. Fidelis says he's mostly actually achieved what he set out to do. When he arrived here, there was only one straggling rose in the cloister garth, and that had black spot. Roses are delicate, picky, they need understanding. He wanted to fill the cloister garth in June with as much fragrance as the chapel full of incense at High Mass. He feels his work is almost done. He says his life is about dedication – training and pruning its rambling habit to run along the structures of the faith. He says his last words will be a prayer for the Lord Jesus to pilot him safely home, and tha he may stay at his Lord's side, in his presence, for ever.

Brother Prudentius sits with his right hand cupped behind his ear and his face screwed up in concentration, listening to this. He's getting deaf and Fidelis hasn't got many teeth left, but it matters to hin tremendously to hear what his brother has to say.

When he's properly ascertained that it's his turn to speak now Prudentius tells Brother Cyril that he's learned you have to be patien with your brothers, because some things they never learn – yoursel as well, of course. Even when they're doing their very best, some o their faults they carry with them to the grave. After that you can laug about it; it becomes endearing. Not while they're alive, sadly. Then it' just annoying.

The only achievement he seeks is to retain enough hearing not t be a confounded nuisance, and to bear meekly the pain in his knees Brother Michael gives him medicine, and it helps.

His life, he thinks, is about bearing witness to the possibilities c the gospel – that if you give it a chance, it will do its miracle, it wi heal your soul. And he wants his last words to be the Lord's Prayer, c course, he says.

Brother Cyril, feeling he has been in the presence of somethin profoundly good, thanks them humbly, and asks permission c Brother Conradus to leave his work and go up to his cell to write down while he still remembers.

* * *

"May I sit with you for a little while?"

Brother Felix turns his head to look. Father William, standing in his room where it's easy for Felix to see him from the bed, asks the question so quietly and courteously that he answers, "Yes, Father, of course." Father William has a plant in a pot in his hands.

Felix has been refusing visitors. Brother Cyril called in again, after Vespers yesterday, but he simply couldn't face seeing anyone. He felt so guilty saying no, but he's come to the end of himself. Under Brother Michael's care his back has subsided from agonised to simply sore, and the infirmarian says two more nights in the infirmary and he'll be able to return to normal if he takes things gently. Brother Felix isn't sure what that means. He's worried about it now. What should normal mean? How do you return to normal, taking things gently, if taking things gently isn't what you normally do? He already is as quiet and recollected and painstakingly disciplined as he knows how to be, mortifying the eyes and walking without self-advertisement and modulating his voice and not taking up too much space as he walks along the cloister, and maintaining right conduct in every smallest detail of every aspect of the life. What is gently if not that? What is he allowed not to do? He doesn't understand. He feels the anxiety mounting as he thinks about it. Right now all he wants is to stay in this quiet room for ever, to sleep and sleep, to no longer have to evaluate what is the correct thing to do in all the tiny circumstances of monastic life with its proliferation of customs and requirements and regulations.

Here in the infirmary, Brother Michael has tended to him with meticulous care, assisted by Brother Christopher. They speak little, and quietly, and it calms the jaggedness in Brother Felix's soul. In the afternoon yesterday, Abbot John came to see him (you can't refuse to see the abbot), and talked with him about how to find a way forward.

He surprised Felix by telling him he had once done the exact same thing to his back, for his own reasons. He didn't say anything more about that, except that he understands about the pain, and the shame and embarrassment of going too far. He asked if he might look at the healed scars on Felix's arms from all the accumulated cuts and burns, and then asked him if he could identify what pushes him towards hurting himself. He suggested some different ways to relieve tension when it all gets too much – both less damaging alternatives to cutting, and possibilities for soothing his spirit at times when he is all jangled inside. He didn't stay too long, and Felix found his company unexpectedly healing; understanding and calm, nothing censorious, no threats about having to leave if he kept doing this. Felix has been scared the abbot might tell him he couldn't stay, even though he's taken his solemn vows. But he didn't, although he was very clear that together they had to find a way to help Felix achieve a workable pattern of peace, and find different ways of managing inner turmoil when it came.

And now here's Father William. Because Felix is feeling less crazy and frantic inside today, even though he still needs to lie face down on the bed and let the hurts heal, he says yes, Father William can stay. "That's a nice plant," he adds, politely.

"Yes," says William. "It is actually a really beautiful plant, but as you can see, it needs a bit of care. I thought – if the idea doesn't wear you out, if you aren't already coping with more than you can bear – perhaps you would look after it for us? Would you do that? It needs someone to wash the leaves, and to give it some water; just touch it gently – maybe even talk to it. Plants listen, don't you find? If I put it down here by the window, is that all right? It can live here, or you can keep it in your cell when you're well enough to move back."

Felix is willing to co-operate with this unexpected request, and gives his assent. Father William places the plant very gently on the table by the window, then picks up the chair and brings it across to sit near Felix – but not too near. He settles himself in it. He doesn't speak. The silence lengthens but Felix is surprised that it doesn't feel awkward. He relaxes a little, letting his mind wander. Maybe all Father William intends to do is what he said – sit there.

"You . . . to be honest I've only heard straws in the wind," says Felix, "but you— didn't you . . . did you try to hang yourself, Father?"

It's a shameful thing, a secret thing, and Felix feels anxiety tighten inside him just from asking the question. But Father William sits quietly, his breathing doesn't change, his face is calm. "Yes," he says. "I did."

"Why . . . why did you do that?" Felix asks him timidly.

"Because," says Father William, "life was unbearable." When he says that – unbearable – it comes adorned with some very extreme expletives; though he still doesn't look upset or agitated, just tranquil and quiet. He glances at Felix, momentarily allows their eyes to meet. "I couldn't take any more. The inside of me hurt more than I could stand. I despised myself. I'd had enough. I needed all the intensity of fear to just . . . shut up."

He stops speaking, and sits in silence, his hands loose in his lap; he looks comfortable and at peace.

"That's how I feel sometimes," admits Brother Felix. "When it all builds up and feels tighter and tighter . . . it doesn't hurt if I burn myself or cut myself – though, oh, by heaven, it does afterwards. But just for a little while it brings relief."

Father William nods thoughtfully, and says nothing for a moment. Then, "When you say that it all builds up," he says, "what does? What's the 'it'?"

"Oh . . . it goes round and round. The expectations that I'll know, that I'll get things right, that I'll never get anything wrong. The expectations that I'll know what to say and do, where to sit, what expression to have on my face, what page to be on . . . everything. And that I will be pure in heart and holy in my conduct, and able to subdue the clamour of intrusive thoughts."

William listens carefully, takes this in. "Those . . . whose expectations are they?" he asks, with no challenge in his voice, just sounding as if he wants to know. "Are those your expectations or someone else's?"

Felix thinks about this. "I – I can't really be sure," he says. "It just seems to be so important to get everything right all the time, and also to be righteous – going beyond being right, to be pure in heart and trustworthy in my practice of personal holiness." Then he moves his head to see Father William better. "Did you always hurt inside?" he asks. "What made it like that?"

"I think I became what people told me I was," William says. "Worthless. Stupid. Filth. Scum. The devil's piss. A blood clot." He stops. "There was a violence in it that grew into my soul, I think," he says. "I couldn't find myself apart from it. It just turned into . . . me."

He doesn't risk looking at Brother Felix, because everyone says his gaze is so intimidating it's actually terrifying; and he thinks right at this moment it could be very scary indeed. So he just breathes quietly, and sits calmly and looks down at his hands, and lets this opening of himself be its own kind of cutting, and a gift of sorts, to this tortured young man.

"Who said those things to you?" Felix asks him.

"Everybody. But my mum and dad, first of all."

Felix licks his lips. William smells his nervousness. "It's all right," William says gently. "You don't have to talk about your own internal pot shards. It's all right."

There is something in the way he says it that makes Felix believe him – trust him. The words repeat in his head in the quiet room: "It's all right."

"Did they . . . did they hurt you?" the young monk asks.

"Yes. They did."

"I mean . . . physically?"

"Yes. They did."

"And . . . does it still hurt? Inside your mind."

"Yes, it does."

"So . . . what do you do to make it stop?"

"Well," says William, "I've learned to let people see – to let them in. I've learned to take up people's time even when they're busy, and let them be . . . nice to me. I've spent hours and hours talking to Abbot John, and he listens, and he helps. I've learned – this is the really hard one – to ask for help."

"I don't think I could do that," says Felix decisively.

"No? Unless, might that be exactly what you've done? Might it be a way to communicate that you . . . I don't know . . . take responsibility, maybe. That you feel terrible about it. But that you aren't bad, just under so much pressure you couldn't contain it. Maybe to show us it's suffering, not sin? Is that . . . is that anywhere near?"

"I don't really think it through like that," says Felix.

Well, maybe you should, goes through William's mind, but he just listens.

"I mean, I think and think, I never stop thinking, thoughts go round and round and round in my head, accusing and full of self-loathing and shame and I feel so dirty, so guilty – I can't stop the thoughts, can't stop, they get tighter and tighter and wind round me harder and harder and I get—"

Slowly, gently, without looking into his eyes, William leans forward and puts a hand on his shoulder. "I know," he says. "It's all right."

He feels Felix trembling, under his hand. "What about right now?" he asks. "When you feel it closing round you like that? Does it make you want to hurt yourself?"

"Well, it would," says Felix, "but everything feels so bad already, it's all just a jumble of confusion. And . . . when you touched me then, it drew some of the poison out. Like a wick. It let some of it go."

William nods. Just as slowly and gently as he put it there, he withdraws his hand. He knows that what begins as a comfort can turn into unwelcome intrusion.

As the next hour unfolds, inching forward like a man walking a narrow mountain path with a precipitous drop right beside it, he makes slow, cautious progress, draws out from Felix what sets off the anguish, what memories are attached to it, what makes it better, what makes it worse. Making neither recommendations nor suggestions, he just works gently at the knot, helping it loosen up, pulling a few threads free. Something is puzzling him, though. He can feel that he's pulling free some of the edges without getting to the nub of the thing. There's something he's missing. Eventually, he feels Felix quite suddenly crash into complex exhaustion.

"I'll get you some milk and honey," he says, "and you can have a little sleep."

"What about that plant, though?" Felix asks him, with a sudden, very evident, arousal of anxiety. "What did you say I'm supposed to do for it? What does it need? What have I got to remember?"

William, who has stood up, looks across at the plant, then looks down at Felix, contemplating him. "The thing is," he says, "it will be all right because we will help you. We'll do it together. The main thing you have to do is just look at it and see that it is beautiful. There's no need to worry. I'll get your milk and honey. I'll be back in a minute."

I hope to God the damned thing doesn't die, he thinks as he walks along the passage to get Felix his drink. The plant was Brother Michael's idea. As he's heating the milk and stirring in the honey, Michael comes into the room to stand beside him. "How did you get on? Did that go all right? By heaven, William, you look exhausted!"

"I am," says William. "Let me just take him this. I'll come back and tell you how far we got, when I've settled him."

He takes the drink through and waits while the young monk slowly and cautiously moves himself into a sitting position, thanks him, and drinks it. He gives William back the cup, thanking him again, wiping his mouth with his hand in a way that reminds William of a child. He glances up. "Thank you," he says again, and eases himself slowly back down onto the bed.

"I feel so tired, Father," he says, and moves his head so he can see William's face, read his expression.

"I know," says William quietly. "I know."

When he says that, Brother Felix feels something inside him relax, not for long maybe, but at least for now. He knows he will be able to go to sleep. He closes his eyes. William stands there, holding the cup, and he prays. His spirit explores into the space, feeling for understanding and insight, for what's eluding him to be made clear. Silently he prays for the block to move, for the pain to dissolve, for the soul to heal, for the grip to lessen, for the knot to untangle, for peace, for ease, for relief. He prays and prays and prays. He feels the lad falling into sleep, feels the soul expand golden and light and slip out of the body into its temporary freedom. And still he prays, in the chance offered by this time of unconsciousness, for Christ to act, for the Spirit to come, for this life to be healed, for release, for a viable pathway, for a way to open. He prays on and on until he shakes with weariness as the power that never diminishes courses through him and through him into Felix's sleeping body, and he lets it flow. He sinks down into the chair again, still holding the cup, still praying, still pushing on . . . Come, Lord Jesus, come, Lord Jesus . . . there is no power but God . . . I bless you with the love of the Lord, I bless you with the love of the Lord, I bless you with the love of the Lord . . . oh, God, shift this thing. Oh, Jesu, come here and help . . . please . . . please . . . help me to see, help me to understand, help me to put my finger on what's troubling him. On into silence, down deep, following Christ down into the hell-harrowing depths his soul descends to find the child who is so gripped by fear and paralysed by shame and guilt, and lead him back up to the light, to where he can breathe easily and is not terrified by shades mocking him. In the name of Jesus Christ, under his eye and by his authority, I set you free, his soul commands. In the name of Jesus.

Come, Lord Jesus . . . oh, Jesu . . . help him . . .

Then, in the room that is this infirmary cell but where the whole cosmos has gathered, Brother Michael is at his side. "He'll be all right, Will," he says softly. "Look, he's sleeping soundly. Come on, now, you're worn out. All will be well."

And William's soul, standing in the name of Jesus, in the overlay of heaven and Earth, the place where stars move and speak, feels Brother Michael's name beside him, realises that Michael has been invested and enrobed in the name of the archangel, so that when he speaks he brings strength as well as gentleness. "Come on, now," Michael says again. "You've done enough." He takes the empty cup out of William's hands.

Getting wearily to his feet and feeling his soul realign with his body, so that this is just an ordinary room again, William hopes it is so. What's the point of being here at all, if not to make things better when they are all broken and jagged, help to knit the wounds of the world and ease the pain? He looks down at Brother Felix, fast asleep.

"Thank you," he says, speaking quietly so as not to wake him. "Shall I wash that cup? It'll be all sticky with honey."

"No," says Michael, "I will. Come on, now." And, of course, what an archangel tells you, you do. "We live in more than one dimension, don't we?" he says to William as they walk along the passage together. "I suppose that's what the Mass is always saying to us – look, this bread, this wine, this ordinary food; these brothers of yours, this oil, this water, this linen, this old friend who stands vested at the altar, through them heaven breathes. Even the light that streams through the east window is saying 'this, but more than this'. And yet there was nowhere I ever saw it plainer than in the infirmary. I think you've done him good, Will. I can feel it in my bones."

* * *

Brother Michael doesn't always make it to Vespers because it coincides with one of the busiest times in the infirmary day. Part of his responsibility as a monastic infirmarian is to so plan things that a space opens up when it's time for the Office – because his foremost priority is the worship of God. Around the holy, the mystery, the beauty of the infinite, his life must centre and organise itself. Everything else, even the pressing needs of the aged and infirm, must bow to that in reverence and respect. But there is a human dimension to his life as well as a heavenly one, so he doesn't always get there despite his best efforts.

Today, things run smoothly and go well. Today, he is in chapel – not sliding in at the absolutely last moment before the abbot gives the knock, but enough in advance to compose his thoughts and find the place in the breviary. He feels good about this, and he relishes the sense of order and peace that arises from it.

As Vespers closes with the familiar petition that our evening prayer may arise before the throne of mercy, and the blessing of God come down upon us, so that now and forever his grace may help and save us, Michael's heart responds *amen and amen and amen*. He sits down again after the final blessing is said, and stays with that image of prayer rising and mercy falling reminding him of rainfall – the mist that arises from the sea, the dew that falls from the clouds above the mountain-top, the rain that falls on the grateful earth and the moisture that steams up from it in the sunshine. Prayer and mercy and blessing . . . the autumn rains that clothe the land with nourishment and fruitfulness. He feels the gladness of life course through him, and he prays for the men in his care with their different needs, the men who work alongside him giving of their best, his abbot and the brothers of his community, the young men in the novitiate still making up their minds, Brother Cyril making his book of their common life.

The brethren are dispersing, hungry for their evening meal, as he sits thinking. He has to go, because, though supper is finished in the infirmary, there are still some loose ends to tie off before the day is done. But his abbot crosses the aisle and stops by his stall. "All well?" he asks. "I'm sorry, I meant to come in and see Felix again today, and just didn't manage to fit it in. How is he?"

These men, they are such good friends. Michael looks at him with affection. "You'd be pleased," he says. "William spent an age with him this afternoon, and made immense progress. He says he prayed for him and tried his best to build on the foundation you laid, helping him find a way forward. And when I left them after supper, I thought Felix looked ever so much better. It'll be the work of a lifetime, of course, to be realistic; but today has been a step in the right direction."

Father John listens, nodding, impressed. "You put your finger on it, asking that William be sent to the infirmary, didn't you? It's working out well."

Brother Michael smiles. "I think he might be kind, but that's not quite the word for it. It's something else. He is," he says, "uncommonly astute."

Chapter Thirteen

It's important, Brother Cyril feels, not to restrict what he's doing to only a few of the brothers – the younger ones, or those in key posts, or those who are more visible, or even just easier to talk to. He wants this to be the book of everyone here.

Even so, it's with trepidation that he sets out when his chores in the kitchen are done, to speak with Father Paul in the infirmary.

Brother Michael has explained to him that Father Paul can no longer speak. He sits up in a chair, and he seems to enjoy his food, but other than that he appears to have become unreachable. Brother Cyril sent him his own piece of parchment with the questions on, so that he wouldn't be left out, he'd be the same as everyone else, and Brother Michael seemed touched and pleased that Father Paul had been included in this way. But Brother Cyril can't imagine how the encounter will go. Sometimes, he has discovered, it can be better not to look too far ahead – not to project hopes and fears onto whatever's happening next. So he does his best to keep his soul gathered in one place – this place, now, where he actually is – rather than letting it go galloping ahead of him into unknown reality. With this in mind he walks along looking at the birds and the leaves turning gold and falling, the majestic clouds and the God-rays of sun slanting through. His attention caught by its chattering, he looks away up at a squirrel watching him from the roof of the infirmary wood store. That makes him smile – Father William was absolutely right about squirrels, he's noticed since.

Then he comes round the low wall into the herby scents and casual peace of the infirmary garden. He recognises Father Clement and Brother Paulinus sitting out in their chairs, but not Father Gerald today. The two who have braved the cold are well swaddled in shawls and wearing hats that come down over their ears, because the wind is from the north-east today. On a low stool, chatting to the old men, is Father William, who looks up at his approach, and stands to greet him.

"Hello," he says. "Father Paul's in his room. You can see him by yourself if you want to, but you won't get much sense out of him, bar a miracle. Brother Michael said the most sensible thing would be if one of us stayed with you. Brother Michael and Brother Christopher are busy with Father Gerald's enema – it takes two to get him in and out of the bath, and he needs help with washing. So I'm sorry to have to tell you, but you've got me again – unless you think a further dose might prove to be fatal."

Brother Cyril, though he is genuinely amused by the wry humour, also asks himself what underlies it. He has a hunch this man might have learned a habit of bracing himself, to deflect the rejection lifelong experience has taught him to expect. Maybe, however indomitable he looks, he needs affirmation like anyone else. So, "Thank you ever so much," he says. "It was a shame you were called away from our conversation the other day – I was so enjoying hearing what you had to say, and I didn't manage to thank you at the time. You left me with a great deal to think on, and what a good thing you'd got the last question answered before you were needed. It must be hard to finish anything sometimes, in the infirmary, I'd guess – similar to the kitchen, but more so. Those of us who work there flatter ourselves we aren't incontinent or demented! Er . . . that is . . . I don't mean you . . . or well, anyone in particular . . ." Worried that he has been unkind and tactless, and that Father Clement undoubtedly heard if not Brother

Paulinus, he looks anxiously at Father William, who is observing his consternation, amused and unperturbed.

Concerned to move on from his blunder, Cyril adds, "Oh – and thank you for the note you pushed under the door of my cell about Father Gerald and Brother Paulinus. That was really helpful. And yes, it would be perfect if you can help me with Father Paul, otherwise I doubt I'll get anywhere."

It takes some courage on his part, at the end of this breathless speech, to feel those intelligent eyes evaluating him. Now he thinks he might be the one who needs reassurance. But he takes heart from that faint gleam of a smile warming Father William's perceptive face.

"Come in then," says William. "Father Clement, ring for me if you need something, or even if you start to feel too cold. The bell's just there, strung from the arm of your chair in the usual place. And you, Brother Paulinus." He pauses, and says very clearly and a little louder (but not shouting), "Did you hear me, Brother Paulinus? I'm going indoors with Brother Cyril here, to Father Paul. Ring your bell if you want me." Brother Paulinus waves his hand in acquiescence and farewell, and Brother Cyril follows Father William indoors.

It's restful in Father Paul's room. The window is ajar even on this chilly day, to freshen the air, and he has a blanket tucked in over his knees in the chair where he sits, and a shawl wrapped round his shoulders. Everything is tidy and clean, and someone has left a small posy of colourful leaves and berries from the garden, in a small green jug on the night stand by his bed. Now Cyril has actually met Brother Thaddeus and Brother Robert, he sees the abbey crockery differently – notices each piece, and how it is shaped, and which glaze is used, and that it isn't red.

"Hello, Father Paul," William says. "Brother Cyril's come to see you. Sit yourself down on the stool there, Brother Cyril. I can perch here on his bed."

Brother Cyril obediently sits down, and he looks at Father Paul.

"Hello," he says, tentatively reaching out to take Father Paul's hand in his. There is no response, no answering pressure to his hand, the old monk just sits chewing rhythmically, his face blank and his eyes staring unwaveringly at nothing. But when Brother Cyril looks round towards the bed for guidance, he thinks Father William looks pleased with him. He wonders what to do next. He gently squeezes Father Paul's hand, and lets it go.

"Father Paul," says William, "used to be our precentor. One of the things he learned, therefore, was the structure of music. He learned the beauty of chant that creates a building within the building, the ethereal architecture of the nursery of the soul. He is a priest, so as well as the regular theology of monasticism, he was formed in the ministry of the sacraments, and took his theological education deeper – as perhaps you will, depending on your sense of call and our abbot's evaluation of it. So, you might say Father Paul's spirit walked out beyond the confines of this Earth, into the airy realms of music and exploring deep into the caverns of the holy. He learned to do that. He's stopped learning now, we think. He's concentrating on teaching *us* – about silence and simplicity and slowness; the essential things every human being needs to know. Father Paul is helping *us* to learn. If you can find space in your book to say so, even just a footnote or a margin note, I think that would not be out of place – but it's your book, so yours is the choice and the decision.

"I have a feeling that what Father Paul would like to achieve is the creation of peace. We try to help him in that endeavour. He doesn't do well with a lot of activity and bustle around him. He likes to sit just quietly, in the garden or in his room. We try to help him achieve that peace his soul yearns towards. He likes porridge with honey a good deal more than pease pudding or regular vegetable pottage, and he's quite enthusiastic about stewed apple. But I think it would be stretching the truth to say he would like to achieve anything in that direction – to express a preference or make a choice; yes, he eats it, but so do we all. Peace is what I think he wants to achieve.

"What he would like his life to be about? Given that he's eighty-six now and has lived here since he'd just turned nineteen years old, I think it would be fair to say he'd be pleased to know we could see his life has been all about faithfulness. He's worn out three abbots and he's doing his best with the fourth. Faithfulness shines from Father Paul's life; what a distance he's walked.

"I think we may already know what his last words might be, because of something Brother Michael remembers him saying when he inadvertently trod on his toe one morning three years ago. But I also think it would not assist any kind of edification you had in mind, to include it in your book. I'll tell you what he said if you like, or we can just leave it. There will be words spoken over him though, probably by either Father John or by me, when his ship makes ready to leave the harbour and the wind lifts his sails. Whichever one of us it is, we will make the holy sign of the cross upon him, and ask the Lord to have mercy on him, absolving him from every earthly sin – *quidquid deliquisti*, as the prayer book says. And then the peace he has striven for will come, to make sense of everything, make it all complete."

He stops talking, looks enquiringly at Brother Cyril with one eyebrow raised, not a trace of self-indulgence or sentimentality in his face. "I hope that's of some use," he says. "You'll have to be the judge of that. Father Paul certainly isn't going to tell us."

Brother Cyril watches with some surprise the formal courtesy with which Father William then makes his farewell to Father Paul as they leave his room. It has more the feeling of a junior monk parting from his abbot than a carer leaving an old man lost in dementia to rest. Father William promises to return later, and thanks Father Paul for his time. He makes a small bow of respect before he goes.

* * *

Passing through the kitchens on his way through to his magical chamber built onto the back of the eastern range, pleasingly enclosing the garden to some extent, Brother Walafrid the herbalist pauses to invite Brother Cyril – who is taking apart a chicken to go in the stew – to come and see him and Brother Giles later on, in the afternoon.

Brother Cyril is curious to see the herbalist's workshop, and takes up the invitation eagerly. It's a fair-sized space, with every nook and cranny used to the full. Here, they make oils and inks and glue, candles and medicines, salves and poultices; they've even had a go at putting together some incense on one occasion when the sacristan forgot to order it in. Every inch of the place has shelves and boxes and chests, stoppered jars and vials of forest glass, cups and crucibles, pestles and mortars, cheesecloths washed and folded and neatly stacked for straining. And it smells heavenly. But at the same time earthy. Wholesome and gloriously fragrant.

Brother Walafrid had forgotten Brother Cyril would be coming to see him, and he's started making some candles because they've harvested all the honey now, so the wax is in. When he looks up and sees Brother Cyril appear in the doorway, Brother Walafrid apologises profusely. He indicates a stool, set by the workbench. "Sit yourself down, lad. I'm so sorry, will you mind if we work as well as talk? That all right? Bless you. Very well, then."

Cyril is more than happy to watch them in their rhythm of work, dipping the plaited and weighted linen threads suspended from the paddle, letting the layers of wax build up then cool off. Besides, it's cosy in here with the brazier burning under the pot of wax – very welcome, it's dismal outside – and the warmth enhances and deepens the pervasive herbal fragrance. He looks at them, their habits protected by linen aprons crusty with wax, their faces flushed from working over the fire. Walafrid, short and dark and stocky, eyes shining from his round and cheery face, looks like a gnome, Cyril thinks. Brother Giles, whom he knows better because he comes to help Brother Richard with the laundry most weeks, is taller, but has the same easy, contented air.

As he sits watching them working deftly together, Brother Giles asks him to jog his memory about the questions. "Just start us off," he says, "and then it'll all come back."

So Cyril reminds them of their first question, and Brother Walafrid says, "The main thing I've learned during my time in this abbey is what they call the discipline of joy. It is absolutely essential to be happy. It's the first thing you have to put into the mixture. We *have* had miserable men here, but their presence didn't help anyone, not even themselves. We just had to put up with them. It's not selfish to be happy, it's the greatest gift you can bring to the community. If, as time goes by, you find you aren't happy here, for God's sake give us all a break and go somewhere else. Don't pass up happiness, don't feel guilty for reaching for it; grab it in armfuls, luxuriate in it. Then, once you have happiness as your basic ingredient, you have to add to it the discipline of joy. Because there *will be* days when you feel wretched or overwhelmed, ashamed or bewildered or just downright exhausted; of course there will. You protect your happiness then with the discipline of joy, the oil of gladness. It is the conscious, confident habit of turning again and again to your happiness, nurturing it and nourishing it with whatever means you find at your disposal – rest, food, music, a nice evening walk, the company of men you like, time with the horses, penmanship or woodwork – anything that lifts your spirits and makes you feel good. Do it. Take responsibility for your own happiness; that's the discipline of joy. Learning to do that is a non-negotiable essential. Wouldn't you say, Brother Giles?"

His assistant heartily assents to this. "Aye, indeed. And with that, I've found for myself, it helps to go gently. That's something I've learned; to handle anything that comes your way with a gentle touch. Be it laundering sheets or gathering herbs or anything you do – and the same goes for how you handle yourself, your body and your soul. Be gentle. Be good-humoured. Take your time. Be kind. There's no place here – or anywhere – for harshness and impatience. They're counter-productive, they waste time in the end. Go gently, lad, in how you pass through life. Even if you have something decisive you need to do, something firm that must be said, even then, don't be rough or punitive, go easy, be gentle. When it comes to how you treat your brothers, but also in the way you treat yourself – you are your own brother, if you see what I mean. Think of your soul as your younger brother, and treat him gently. I've learned that it helps."

They lift out the paddle, set it on the stand to dry, lift the next one in. The layers are building up nicely and the wax in the pot is going down. Soon the altar candles will be done and they'll move on to the next size down, the ones that go in the frater.

"About what we want to achieve," Brother Walafrid says, "heart and soul I'm here to create beauty and healing. In fact, beauty is one of the things that heals us. It needs to be appropriate, too. When we make the oil for our abbot – the one he rubs on his body at the end of the day – we put together something specially for him. There's meaning in a name, so we use hazelnut oil as the base for him. He needs strength and cheerfulness and encouragement for the work he does, so we put in rosemary and clary sage, lemon balm and lavender and hawthorn – and a few drops of rose absolute, because why not? It isn't from our roses, of course – we grow some, but not enough. This comes to England on a ship from . . . er . . . a hill country in the eastern reaches of the world, I think. Where the Magi came from, or somewhere near that. A place of stars and mystery – and roses in profusion, obviously."

Brother Giles listens to this, and Cyril loves the expression on his face; not exactly smiling but profoundly happy. "What I want to achieve," he says, "is what you might describe as plenty, abundance maybe. None of us ever knows when the Lord will call us home. On the day I die, I want to leave things so that no one goes short of anything they need. I want to be sure the shelves and the chests are well stocked, so that I leave provision and continuity behind me – no gaps, no consternation, just flowing peace. So they hardly notice I've gone, because there's a new man in the obedience before the stores are used up."

The altar candles are built up and ready to be moved to one side now. Brother Giles picks up another paddle, adds new threads and ties on the weights. The threads are of the same length as for the tall candles obviously, because they have to reach to the bottom of the tank of wax; it'll just be a longer length left over at the top.

"What I'd like my life to be about," says Brother Walafrid, "is what you might call holy imagination. Our time on Earth is short, Brother. We have no time to waste. I am here, I suppose, to bring something to life that no one else can do, that has never been seen before. I walk in the footsteps of all who went before me, but I bring the holy spark of my soul's particular fire. I mustn't withhold it. I am necessary. To know that is not pride, it is humility. God called me to be here. I am here to bring into the material plane the power of the Spirit that pulses in me. To do that is an exercise of imagination."

Brother Cyril has no idea what he means, but thinks it sounds somehow exciting and wonderful. Brother Giles chuckles. "Aye," he says. "Have you seen his cell? You haven't? You've missed a treat. Take him to see, Walafrid, when we're done in here. I should think there'll be time before Vespers."

Giles says he thinks of life as something like weaving, where you take all the separate threads and make them one thing. "My life has been about learning the warp and the weft of this community. A thread may break, and yet it can be mended because the others hold together. Make it pliable, the holy fabric of your life," he says. "Make it supple, the way you weave it all together into one. Make it airy and light and warm and soft. Who wants something scratchy and stiff folded round them?"

Cyril wonders what this would mean in practice, but they've moved on. "My last words," says Brother Walafrid, "I don't know . . .

I think, you see, our souls are made of golden light. When I've seen a man die, seen his soul leave, it was so – like amber-gold oil with light shining through, light inside it. 'We have this treasure in jars of clay,' the apostle says. I think we are like stoppered jars of golden oil, like that oil I told you about, that we make for Father John. When we die, the Lord lays us down and takes out the stopper. The golden oil flows out into the earth, you see it go, but the fragrance arises to heaven. That'll do me instead of words."

Brother Giles lifts the paddle up dripping from the tank. Cyril enjoys watching the confident expertise with which he sets it on the stand, not knocking or smudging anything, just getting it accurately right. Walafrid lifts down the dried one and dips it into the wax.

"I think when it's my time to go," says Brother Giles, "if I feel my strength ebbing, what I'd love best of all is if whoever is looking after me will take me outside. Even if it's the hard frost of winter, oh, I'd like to see one more time the moon and the stars. If it's raining, then to feel it one more time coursing down my face. If it's a sunny afternoon, one last time to smell the herbs and hear the bees among the flowers. And if it's evening, then to hear the blackbird sing. I shan't want to speak. Only to look and listen. I love this Earth, Brother Cyril, but heaven is my home."

As they finish up making their candles, Brother Giles assures Brother Walafrid he can complete the task, and urges him to take Cyril to see his cell. So Walafrid takes off his apron and together they go round by the reredorter and up the back stairs to the cells. Brother Walafrid's is in the row against the south-facing wall, so it gets the afternoon light, warm and golden. Brother Walafrid makes nearly all their ink. Sometimes he sets just a tiny amount aside. Over the thirty-four years he's been here, he has little by little illuminated every inch of the walls of his entire cell. There are flowers and leaves and bunches of herbs, all immediately identifiable, intertwined with rambling roses in bloom and climbing vines bearing grapes. There are rabbits and squirrels and deer, foxes and badgers and field mice. There are toadstools, birds flying and singing, the moon in its different phases and constellations of stars. There are depictions of monks about their daily work – milking a cow, chopping wood, one carrying a lantern and one bearing a basket of bread. There are trees with apples and plums, and sheaves of corn – and in among it all small phrases of the psalms and prayers that shape Brother Walafrid's life, complete with capitals to begin them ornamented with curlicues and picked out in different hues. The whole room glows with colour and imagery. Here and there some parts are gilded, just touched with a glint of gold, from some loose leaf he gleaned from the floor in the scriptorium when he took up their ink. He makes the gesso and size for the gilding, Cyril realises; obviously he sometimes has a smidgen of that going spare as well.

It's like actually standing inside Brother Walafrid's imagination. He's even done the ceiling, painting directly onto the wood of the rafters – and this roof painting likewise has details picked out with touches of gold. "How the heck did you get up there?" Brother Cyril gasps.

"Well, we do have ladders, Brother," says Brother Walafrid.

"It's . . . oh, it's beautiful!" says Cyril, boggling, swivelling round to look at it all, amazed. "It . . . I'm astonished. I mean, I wouldn't have guessed you'd be allowed to do this." "Oh, I'm not," says Brother Walafrid cheerfully. "I've served under three abbots here, Brother, and if any of them have ever been in here, well they've never mentioned it. But of their charity, they never asked me to move to a different cell."

Chapter Fourteen

Brother Cyril regards their precentor with great respect – possibly even awe. He's known him since he was a schoolboy, but now he sees him every day. He observes Father Gilbert's dignified bearing and patrician features as he stands to conduct his singing group at Mass. He listens not only to the content of the reading at mealtimes, but also to Father Gilbert's erudite tones in the delivery of it. He is fairly sure that however many years he lives in this place, he's never going to end up like Father Gilbert. In some ways he feels privileged to come under his tutelage and influence like this; in a different mood he feels merely unable to relate to him. But he has to this morning, because the novice master has released him from his studies to go through the mealtime readings with the precentor. It's Brother Cyril's turn to read, and he's only done it once before, so Father Gilbert is still taking the precaution of preparatory oversight and advice.

Brother Cyril reads well, as it happens. He doesn't stumble over words, he can read ahead easily, his pronunciation of the Latin is good when it's required. So the practice is not as extensive as Father Gilbert sometimes considers necessary. They are finished well before the chapel bell rings for the midday Office.

"Your book, Brother Cyril," enquires the precentor with refined courtesy, "is it coming along well? Are you finding our individual contributions helpful and interesting?"

Cyril assures him that he is – and then grasps that this is a hint for him to offer the invitation he therefore hastily supplies: "Are you ready to share your own answers with me, Father?"

He feels irritated with himself, realising that he's actually imitating the way Father Gilbert speaks, and earnestly hopes the man doesn't think he's making fun of him. But as the conversation moves serenely on, he wonders if in fact everyone starts to speak like Father Gilbert around Father Gilbert – so the precentor maybe never finds out that's not how they normally talk.

"Indeed, Brother," comes the reply. "If you feel this would be a good time. Shall we sit down?"

They're standing in the frater where Cyril's been practising, and he thinks any time soon Brother Richard will be clattering about with knives and spoons and bowls of fruit and pickles, but he also thinks a novice shouldn't be arguing with the precentor. So he simply acquiesces, and they sit down at one of the long tables opposite one another.

"You asked what I have learned."

For the first time Brother Cyril feels both foolish and ashamed at putting such a question. Here is this scholarly, highly intellectual, silver-haired senior monk, mature in years and mind and monastic experience. *What have you learned? How could I have had the temerity to even ask him?*

But he realises Father Gilbert doesn't take it as impudence; far from it. He's been thinking about it honestly and seriously. "Well," he says, "we go on learning, it never stops, which is just as it should be. But if I could put my hand on one lesson that has come round many times for me, it would probably be learning the wisdom of curbing my enthusiasm. I made the mistake, when I entered monastic life, of assuming there is a difference between monks and people of the world but within the community the brethren would think alike. Without giving it any real thought, I took it for granted they would essentially be all the same kind of people. Not only that, but I reverted to this fundamentally and obviously flawed misconception again and again. They're not . . . not the same at all. The men within the community are as different from one another as from men outside the community, and as men outside the community are from each other. Frankly, we're as different from one another as oxen from bullfinches, as garlic from peaches. In fact, I can think of brothers here who are decidedly and outstandingly unique. I expect you can too, but we won't linger on that. One minor example is that my ideas about the importance of the kind of music we sing and the prominence that should be given to it, is profoundly at variance with our abbot's – and he is my superior, and a wise and holy man. I bow to his judgement; actually, I have to. So I have learned to curb my enthusiasms, because not everyone shares my views and interests. I continue to learn new variants of this particular lesson every passing year.

"Then, you asked what I would like to achieve. I hesitated about this. I wanted to hide the truth from you, but I have concluded that would be deceitful. What I'd like to achieve, Brother, if God in his goodness should grant it, is to make this abbey a centre of musical distinction; a shining beacon of monastic chant, a pinnacle of excellence. That's not so we can show off, or look down on others; it's because it's worth doing, because music heals the soul and lifts the spirit and builds community and incarnates beauty. So that's what I'd like to achieve.

"And what I would like my life to be about? Above all, empowerment and encouragement. I have learned that one of the most pernicious and damaging things in life is discouragement. You can die of it. I mean that literally. And we are here to comfort and encourage one another. What our lives are for is to improve the life of somebody else. Young men are sent to me to learn to sing, and learn to read. Some of them are absolutely brilliant from the outset; others are so awfully bad at it there's a temptation to write them off as entirely hopeless. But the reality is that if you give them six months and a great deal of steady encouragement, they can do it – they can read, both words and music, and at the same time; they can sing, and in tune and in time. In some cases it feels like the nearest thing imaginable to a miracle. Making it happen is what my life is about. That is, more than anything else I do, a source of joy.

"Now then, my last words. I confess to you, Brother Cyril, that though I believe firmly in God, and I have an unshakeable conviction in the afterlife, partly *because* of that I am afraid of dying. I am not perfect. I am a sinful man. I don't know how I could hold up my head before the Lord Christ, my Judge, and look him in the eye. My knees would be knocking uncontrollably. So, though I feel ashamed of this really, I think my last words on this Earth would not be for someone else, but words of Jesus repeated for the comfort they bring *me*, that I think I'll sorely need. 'Let not your hearts be troubled, neither let them be afraid.' I'm hoping that will do the trick, and help me lay down my life in peace, when the time comes for me."

Brother Cyril is most heartily grateful and glad that it's not until this precise moment that Brother Richard comes in to lay up ready for lunch. He does his best, but he is not the very quietest of monks. In fact Brother Benedict says if you imagine a dawn chorus of knife-grinders, that wouldn't even come close. The fraterer has to fulfil his obedience – of course he does – but Cyril is really pleased that he had the chance to listen properly to Father Gilbert, who, with a slightly pained smile and a look of determined restraint, offers him a little bow, mouths, "Thank you," and gets up to go.

* * *

It'll soon be time for Compline. Darkness has fallen. This is the time of year when the coming of winter is most deeply and regretfully felt, when the long days of the light still linger in the memory, the dry, warm days of summer when bare feet in sandals are enough and no one needs to wear a heavy cloak, and the path isn't strewn with puddles to catch the unwary, and you don't get poked in the eye by an apple tree as you hasten along to chapel in the dark once the aged residents of the infirmary are in bed.

Brother Michael is taking the doses round to settle the old men to sleep and see them through the hours of the night free of pain. Brother Christopher is swabbing down the supper tables and sweeping the floor and clearing up the work bench in the dispensary. Father William goes to check on Brother Felix, who is healing well, but is still caught in a loop of anxiety and anguish, still hanging on to the safety of his infirmary room. The door being ajar, William quietly walks in, then stops. He sees that Brother Felix, lying on his bed with his back turned to the door, is far from asleep but entirely occupied. His presence is inappropriate, evidently. He very cautiously retreats. He's often glad he mastered the art of walking silently. It wasn't the moment to intrude. The infirmary offers even less privacy to anyone than the rest of the abbey. People need a refuge, to be left in peace, be given some solitude to relieve the needs of the body. He occupies himself for a few minutes plumping the cushions used for padding the old men's chairs, to give Brother Felix some personal space. But it's nearly time for Compline and everything needs to be done, so he goes back, this time knocking distinctly on the young man's door.

"Do you need anything for pain, Brother Felix?" he asks. "Is your back giving you trouble?"

Brother Felix, moving much more easily after these few days of healing and rest, adjusts his clothing and moves into a sitting position then swings round, bringing his bare feet to the floor, to make himself more respectfully available to a senior monk. He looks up at Father William, who meets his gaze with immaculate neutrality and an enquiring lift of the eyebrows. "Are you comfortable? Can I get you anything?"

"Father," mumbles Felix, "I—" There then follows something quite incomprehensible, as Felix sits there before him, positively shaking, speaking very fast and extremely quietly.

William frowns, wondering if he's missed something, if the lad has done some further injury to himself that is not immediately apparent. Nothing he saw before seems to him to warrant this. "I'm sorry – what?" he says.

Felix, his expression utterly wretched, entirely mortified, looks as if he wished he was anywhere else on Earth. His hand fiddling nervously with a fold in the blanket, he lowers his eyes. He cannot look at Father William now, but he finds it within himself to tell him – absolutely consumed with shame – what has happened, what he has done, and William's face clears; oh – it *was* only that. He lets him say it, listens unperturbed. He doesn't look concerned, but he doesn't laugh either. He just listens, but then something else puzzles him. "Yes, but you've done it often enough before, surely?" *You certainly looked as though you knew what you were doing*, he thinks, but rejects that as anything that should pass into verbalisation.

Felix, bending his head to obscure his face from view, nods slowly. "Yes, Father," he says. He won't look up now.

William considers this, contemplates the young man, sitting trembling on the bed in front of him. Then a thought comes to him. He turns back and pushes the door almost shut behind him, then sits down on the chair at the bedside. "Brother Felix," he says, "before you came here – before you took your vows – did you used to cut yourself?"

Felix shakes his head, miserably. This feels worse than any time of confession he's ever endured.

"So . . . all this scourging and burning and cutting . . . that's all because of *this*?"

Again Felix nods. Shrivelling in shame, he cannot bring himself to speak.

"Oh, Lord have mercy – look, Felix – we all do it. We're all human.

We . . . didn't Father Theodore say anything to you about this in the novitiate?"

Felix still won't look up. He brings his hands together, twisting in his lap, the knuckles white. "He said . . . he told us to fix our minds on what is holy," he mumbles. "Because images stay with us. And I tried to do what he said – I really did. He said we shouldn't linger too long over some of the pictures in illuminated manuscripts, just pass on by. I tried to do it right, but the pictures just stay in my mind. Father said we should live in recollection and focus our hearts on prayer, and I do, but . . . somehow it never goes away. I strive and strive to be pure, to mortify my flesh, to fix my mind on what is holy, like he said."

William makes a mental note to have a word with Father Theodore. "Yes," he says, "but you are still a human being, still *made* of flesh. All of us linger on those pictures Father Theodore mentioned – the only variation is how long and which pictures. Not only that, but someone sat there and actually painted them, and, what's more, his abbot signed them off. Probably said to him, 'That's good, lad, how about some for the psalter?' Here in our library, we – well, you probably know. Anyway, the human race is only here because of the urges and needs of the flesh. These instincts are present in every man and every woman. The strength of it varies, for sure, but if you ever manage to get rid of yours altogether, come over here and ask to see Brother Michael, because you'll be sick not holy. Your body doesn't stop being what it is because you've made a vow. It's inevitable. It needs release. What I said – we all do it."

Brother Felix still cannot look at him. His head still bent, he timidly ventures to ask, "You? Father Abbot? Father Master?"

"Me, yes, sure," says William. "John and Theodore – well, I imagine so. It hasn't been a topic of conversation. Ask them. They'll tell you. They're honest men."

The door to the room is not quite closed. Behind him, William hears Brother Michael's voice: "Christopher and I are going over for

Compline, Will. Should we wait for you, or . . .?"

William twists round and raises his voice to reply. "You go on," he says. "I might slip in at the back. But don't wait."

As Brother Michael's footsteps recede down the passageway, Felix makes himself look up at William. "*Now* look what's come of it," he says miserably. "Sin upon sin. You should be in church."

William shrugs. "'Where can I go from thy presence?'" he says. "The Lord Jesus is here. The chapel's not a God-sty. Brother Felix, listen to me, it's not carnality you're suffering from, it's scrupulosity. You've got an overdose of religion. It's out of balance. A man needs to be humble enough to accept and live with reality. God *made* you human, and pronounced it good. It's not realistic to try to be more holy than God, is it?" He waits, but there is no response to this. He can see Felix is thinking about it though, sees some of the tension slightly dissipate. The young man has come to trust William enough that somehow he summons the courage then to admit what it is he fears. "Do you think," he says, "Father, do you think – tell me honestly, I can take it – do you think I'll go to hell now?"

The full nature of the problem only now dawns on William. "I'm sorry – can I get this straight? You've been cutting and burning and scourging yourself every time you . . . Jesus, man! What were you thinking? And here in the infirmary there are no scourges and nothing to hurt yourself with, so you haven't been able to punish yourself so you think you'll be thrown into hell?"

"Yes." A whisper is all Felix is capable of.

"Felix," says William, "I think you've got the wrong end of the stick. We are not saved by punishment nor even religion. We are saved by grace. It's an easy mistake to make, but righteousness isn't about being right – it's more about goodness, which comes from kindness. Someone taught me once, years ago now, that the power of God is in mercy more than justice. If there's one thing I've learned, it's that what heals us – our salvation, if you like – is patience and kindness and understanding – that's what grace *is* – not by punitive religiou zeal and savage punishment. It's been one hell of a struggle for me, b I've tried to climb out of hating myself and blaming myself into som workable level of acceptance. I've tried – I mean, I'm still trying, haven't got there yet – to make my life about something that helps m live with myself and make peace with my humanity. Integrate it all."

"So . . ." Felix needs to ask him again, has to be sure. He glanc up, and William thinks he can see hope as well as fear in the haunte face, the harrowed eyes. "Really and truly – honestly – even if I dor do penance, the Lord Christ won't turn me away? I won't be burne in hell?

"*No*," says William firmly. "Absolutely not. You will *not*. I take by doing penance you mean hurting yourself? Cutting, burnin thrashing yourself with a scourge until you bleed? No. Stop it. Just sto You won't go to hell. You will not. I think a far more likely outcome that you'll go to sleep. Don't worry about it, Felix. It's just normal. I all right. Don't feed the thoughts that bother you by giving them you attention. Let them come, let them go, let them be. What you fight ge stronger. Just disregard them."

He sits quietly then, observing Brother Felix, watching the change He sees the young man's hands stop wringing, then stop gripping ar rest still. He sees his shoulders drop a little and his face soften. I hard to tell by candlelight, but he thinks Felix's face looks less taut, le set. The young monk is still not looking at him, but he's just gazin thinking, occasionally blinking. William judges he will be all rig now. He won't try and hurt himself if he's left alone.

William gets to his feet and adds, "Look, give me that cloth c the bed and I'll wash it for you." Felix doesn't move and some of t tension and shame visibly reassert themselves. Even so, William thin if he removes the rag at least it will keep the whole incident priva from further discovery. He steps forward and picks it up from t rumpled blanket, by its corner. "Help yourself to another one any tin you like," he says. "Be at peace. The Lord Christ loves you in all your humanity. He was also human. That's what it means to be Emmanuel."

He hesitates a moment then asks, "Is it all right if I go to chapel? I've missed Compline three times already this week. Father John will be having something to say to me if—"

"Of course! Oh, please!" Felix looks up at him in consternation. "Please, Father! Don't let me keep you! Please don't miss Compline because of me. And – thank you so much. I feel so much better inside, now."

Consciously, using all his soul's observational power, William looks at him, and sees this really is so. With a small nod of satisfaction, "Go to sleep," he says. "Rest easy. Or just sit by the fire if you're wakeful. I'll come back after chapel."

Walking swiftly but going round by the laundry vats to toss the soiled cloth in with other soaking linens, William makes the best haste he can through the darkness. At least, he thinks, the boy didn't start to cry – he'd have been there forever if that had happened. He knows he's outrageously late, but it's understood. It comes with the infirmary work. He hears the chant flowing back and forth across the choir, and makes himself slow his pace to recollected decorum as he comes through into the choir and sits down in the seat for latecomers rather than making himself obtrusive by going through to his stall. Oh, right. They're past the introduction, the confession, the hymn and already at the *gloria* of the psalm. He squashes the nascent thought that it probably wasn't worth coming at all. He closes his eyes. He doesn't need a breviary for this. *Into thy hands, O Lord, I commend my spirit . . . thou hast redeemed us, Lord, thou God of truth . . . Yes . . .* his soul quests into the flow of chant, hungry and thirsty always for the touch of Christ's love, that he knows, that he can feel. *Felix . . .* he thinks *. . . me . . . all of us . . . we are only human . . . for thy love's sake . . . please don't let us go.*

Chapter Fifteen

"Have you got a moment? Is this a good time?"

Father Theodore, setting the benches of his teaching circle back into place in readiness for the next day, and gathering up the music they were working with during the morning, straightens up and turns round at the sound of William's voice. "That sounds ominous," he says. "Has something happened?"

William, standing in the doorway, is still waiting for an answer to his question.

"Oh – yes – come in," says Theodore. "Close the door behind you if it's something private."

William does so, but says, "It's all right, it shouldn't take long."

Theodore gestures in invitation to one of the low stools at the fireside, and they sit down together. Without preamble, William tells the novice master about Brother Felix. "I know he took his solemn vows some time ago—"

"Three years," says Theodore quietly. He has been listening attentively, his face grave.

"Three years, then. He presumably has someone other than you as his confessor?"

"Father Gilbert."

"And he has been under the close care of our abbot since this last round of self-inflicted injury. So I certainly wouldn't want to give you the impression I'm laying at your door any responsibility for his extreme and unrealistic approach to his practice of celibacy. It's more that I wanted to alert you to . . . well, tell you about it in case you might wish to review whatever is your current teaching about Christian chastity."

Theodore sits thinking, without moving, gazing at the floor. "I'm so sorry this has happened," he says. "Thank God he found the insight to see the connection and confide in you."

"I only found out by accident," William responds. "He thought it was what he was supposed to be doing – driving out his demons, so to speak. Doing penance for every lapse. Purifying himself of sin. He's been frightened of damnation. So far as I know, we haven't got anyone else as scrupulous and knotted up inside as Brother Felix, but I just thought we – you – might be well advised to learn from it in case another aspiring saint lands in our midst."

"Yes," says Theodore. "You're absolutely right. Have you spoken to Father John?"

"Not yet. I wanted to see you first, in case what I've just said to you also occurred to him."

"I see. Thank you. That was thoughtful. I'm not sure what to say, William, except that I am so very sorry. It sounds as if I let him down when he was learning under my care. I know how these things can get out of hand – he could have killed himself in the end. It goes beyond all reasonable discipline, becomes immoderate. Oh, God, I'm so sorry. So very sorry."

He glances up at William. "Thank you for telling me."

William shrugs. "Just so you know. For what it's worth, I doubt there's a better novice master in all Christendom than we've got here. If I'd thought you not capable of adjusting to take account of it, I wouldn't have bothered saying anything. I can't see that Felix's obsessive nature can be anyone's problem other than his own, but . . ."

"Yes," says Theodore, "*but* I could have foreseen an obvious area of focus. And I didn't."

William stands up to go. "Don't take it too much to heart," he says. "I didn't think of it, nor did Michael, nor did John. You're a good novice master, Theodore. The best."

After he's gone, Theodore swivels round on his stool, leaning his shoulder and his head against the warm stones of the fireplace, gazing down into the embers glowing red. He prays for Brother Felix, for the young men presently in his care, for healing, for a sound and positive expression of monastic celibacy, for tenderness and vulnerability, for warmth and human wholeness. He prays for forgiveness. Eventually, when he can bring himself to it, he gives thanks for Father William's perspicacity. Then he closes his eyes and just thinks for a while, about how to revise his present teachings on holy chastity.

* * *

Brother Cyril doesn't really know the monks who run the school, at all. He's seen them in chapel and in Chapter and at mealtimes, of course, and formed a sketchy impression of them.

He knows Brother Josephus used to help in the infirmary and sometimes in the kitchen before they settled him full time in the school. This suggests he must be calm, and good around people, and practical. Fairly tall, slender in build, with a mild expression and an air of self-discipline, Brother Cyril has sometimes looked at his lowered eyes and appearance of self-containment, and wondered what lies within.

Brother Cassian is younger; cheerful, with a ruddy face and stocky build. Cyril knows he took his solemn vows only fairly recently – did they say three years ago? Or four? Not long since, anyway. He looks easy-going and approachable.

It was Cassian who came to find Brother Cyril at the conclusion of the midday meal, to say, "We finish school at the end of the morning. In the afternoon we're generally preparing lessons and tidying up and doing the schoolhouse chores. If you have time to come over and see us in our native territory – or we can come up to you in the novitiate schoolroom, whichever suits you best – we could talk through the questions you gave us for your book. Tomorrow, if you like."

Cyril takes the option of going across to the abbey schoolroom. He knows it well, of course; he was brought up in the village, and the parish church is served by the monks of St Alcuins. There's nowhere else for a boy to learn to read and write, except his own home. Cyril and his brother Rory both came here for their lessons back in the days when Father Aelred, already very old even then and long dead now, had been the schoolmaster, assisted at that time by Father Gilbert.

Though you'd expect the abbey school to be located, like most, upstairs in the gatehouse on the absolute periphery of the abbey grounds, to keep the coming and going of worldly – and in this case, possibly noisy – people to a minimum, at St Alcuins the siting is unexpected, but that's because it wasn't always a schoolroom. Built before any of the rest of the abbey to house the monks who came to establish it here, the small building was left just outside the abbey wall, only a few yards to the west, in a patch of open ground roughly defined by an informal accumulation of birch and hawthorn, dog roses and brambles and weeds, trimmed when necessary to keep the school yard clear. An oak tree grows near there too, so old that its hefty roots serve as a seating network in the summer. Now, in the autumn, its falling shower of amber leaves provide material for juvenile entertainment.

There's a door in the abbey wall through which the teachers can come and go, but it's secured on the inside by three very substantial bolts, so they can only get back in if they went out that way. There's a consensus agreement that a door left open, with no watch set, makes the tenants of the abbey close vulnerable to opportunistic intrusion, so the schoolmasters usually settle for taking the long way round through the abbey gatehouse. The school room stands near the road that runs down the hill to the village. In the winter, boys who climb laboriously

up, walking on the frozen grass where feet grip well, make ice slides o
the downhill way home, to the intense irritation of villagers walking
up to Mass at the abbey, and carters bringing produce up the track
After the recent days of intermittent sunshine and heavy rain showers
the way is not a morass of mud, but the ruts have become puddle
reflecting the massy grey of clouds.

A faint drift of smoke rises from a chimney at the end furthes
from the school house door, because there's a fireplace inside it, takin
up most of the wall at the back. It's a surprisingly large one, but that'
because the monks who built it towards the end of the 1100s neede
somewhere to cook as well as get warm and dry in the winter up here i
the North York Moors, for the time it takes to build an abbey – longe
than the life span left to most of them. The whole thing is built o
the same stone as the abbey – no brick, no cruck frame, Romanesqu
vaulting providing the structural ribs to give it strength – and its roo
is tiled with stone, well colonised by beautiful green-gold lichen. Th
floor inside is likewise flagged with stone. It's a simple building bu
in an old-fashioned way, beautiful. Later, when the rest of the abbe
was complete and the monks had settled in, the passing time wit
its changes and innovations brought the opportunity of glazing th
windows. This was not as much of a challenge as it could have bee
It is a simple, practical house, the windows small and square. Nothin
ornate was of relevance for somewhere meant only as a tempora
dwelling. After the St Alcuins community had it glazed they still ke
the original shutters, to close up at night. The building is low an
unsupervised; glazed windows are precious and it would be beyon
imprudent to leave them exposed to chance.

Going in through the sturdy curved arch of the mullioned doorwa
the plain and orderly dispensation of benches and desks is so famili
to Cyril's eye, and the comfortable fragrance of woodsmoke makes
feel like coming home.

"Hello!" Brother Cassian looks up from the schoolmaster's de at the front, where he's filling ink horns in readiness for tomorrow morning's lesson. "Brother Josephus will be back any minute now. He went across to get us some feathers. We're going to show the lads how to make quill pens tomorrow. They don't need them here, as such, because we have the wax tablets, and we can just re-use those as often as we like. But they do need to know how to handle a pen, and to do that they'll have to have practised making one as well as using it. Making ink's a bit more complicated, of course, but if they stay in the neighbourhood they can always come up and get some from us, or just make do with elderberries or blackberries. It's good enough, just fades quicker. Oh – here comes Brother Josephus now."

"So sorry to keep you waiting, Brother," says Josephus as he brings the parcel of feathers wrapped in linen to the master's desk. "Not too long, I hope? I came through the wall gate, to save time. I hope you didn't get soaked going the long way round?"

Everybody should come here, thinks Brother Cyril. *Everyone. Even if they only stayed for half a year, for a summer, anything – just long enough to learn from these men how to talk to people. They are so considerate. So courteous.* He smiles at Brother Josephus. "It was only just coming on to rain, I dodged the raindrops. Thank you for letting me take up your time like this. It feels good to be here again, actually. It's where I learned my letters, as a little lad. With Father Aelred."

"Oh – aye! Father Aelred!" Josephus nods, remembering. Brother Cassian's family live at a greater distance, so he learned to read from his parish priest, and Father Aelred died before he had the chance to get to know him.

"Well, then – shall we sit by the fire?" Brother Josephus pulls the two benches at the back towards the hearth. "It's only embers now, we let it die down; but there's some warmth coming off the stones as well, of course. What would you like us to do, Brother Cyril? Just launch straight in? I love this idea of yours, by the way."

Cassian stoppers the vial of ink, and the last inkwell, setting it securely on its cradle, and comes across to join then, wiping the traces of ink from his fingers onto the skirts of his habit. There's a lot to be said for wearing black.

As they tell him about what they have learned and still want to achieve, Brother Cyril thinks what a good team they make – the natural dignity in Brother Josephus's quiet, well-modulated tones that convey academic learning and personal discipline, and the younger monk's friendliness and easy-going confidence; he can see how well they would work together as schoolmasters.

Brother Josephus feels monastic life has, yes, drawn him closer to God, but also has made him properly acquainted with himself. Self-knowledge, he says, is never comfortable and is sometimes downright painful, but you cannot progress in monastic life without it. And even if you thought you could, your abbot and your novice master would set you straight.

Brother Cassian, listening to this, smiling as he nods his acquiescence, looks at Brother Josephus to check the silence that follows this is not just a pause. Seeing Josephus is waiting for his own contribution, he speaks. "I've been thinking about this – you'll be glad to hear. Out of the usual muddle and chatter of my thoughts, there began to emerge one particular thing. This might sound odd, living as we do in community, and working in the school, but here I've learned the depth and immense strength of solitude. After Compline, when we go into silence and withdraw to our cells, right round through to Chapter the next morning, is – as I have no doubt you'll have noticed for yourself – no short stretch of time. All kinds of things rise up to the surface and take me by surprise. Loneliness, doubt, shame at something I said or did – or didn't do, or forgot – discouragement, even fear sometimes. The night can be long. But it's transformative, too. In the night hours – well, that is to say, I'm often crashed out and snoring, and there's Nocturns in the middle of it, but apart from that – in the silence and the solitude and the light of just the candle in my cell, sometimes I think I have met with the living Christ, I really do. And I think, and I pray. Yes, that's been a really . . . um . . . *significant* and valuable learning for me."

Brother Josephus nods soberly. "Amen," he says.

As they move on to a consideration of what they want to achieve, Brother Josephus speaks of his vision to make a difference in the lives of the village lads. Most of them come from homes where someone might have a rosary but no one will have a missal or a book of Hours. There will never have been reference to philosophy or theology – often not even the homespun variety. Everything they know is conditioned by the practical addressing of physical need; survival. What Brother Josephus wants to achieve for them is a glimpse beyond. He wants to help them lift their gaze for just the shortest while, and discover new and wonderful horizons.

Brother Cassian confesses that though he likes teaching school and loves working with Brother Josephus, he'd also like the chance to try some other areas of work. He's interested in what the cellarer does, and he wonders if Father John might allow him to assist Brother Cormac and learn more about it; but he hastens to emphasise that he is content in his obedience, that he does not question the abbot's decision, and that he knows it will depend on them finding someone else suitable to teach in the school. "It's not for everyone," he says. "Brother Damian was such a good teacher, but he felt very grateful to put it down. He won't be easy to replace. The boys loved him."

Brother Cyril has begun by now to recognise how caution and discretion are handled here. Discussion of other people's inner conflicts is not encouraged unless it's necessary. He's not surprised when Brother Josephus steps in to move the conversation on from Brother Damian to their third question – what they see their life as being about.

"This . . . I think this might surprise you," says Brother Josephus (and he's right, it does), "because I am aware it sounds a little insipid, to say the least. But I think my life is about tradition. Yes, I'm sorry – I know – that's very disappointing, isn't it! Not a man you could learn anything worthwhile from! Heheh. That's probably true, as it happens. I'd better explain or you'll think my soul has atrophied into a stale crust, or something. You cannot put the gospel, the living hope, the redemptive power, the transforming love, the healing light of Christ into any physical thing. You can point to the bread and wine of the Eucharist, to the holy books of the Bible, to the Angelus bell ringing out from our abbey to remind the people to pray – but the meaning of it and the sense it makes is not in the things themselves; that's in the tradition. You can say it is seen in holy lives and in human encounter; well, yes. But *which* human lives? The ones that have been shaped and formed by the tradition.

"Tradition is a flowing river, a current that bears us along. It is the living tradition that makes our lives and all the outward signs of the faith into one seamless continuum with the life of Jesus – both historical and eternal. It's in the tradition that we find one another and discover how to take our place in the cloud of witnesses. Tradition is what carries the living flame of the gospel, passing the torch from hand to hand in each new generation. The tradition isn't merely a commemorative husk. It is alive. And that's what my life is all about."

There's a silence after this. Brother Cassian looks disinclined to speak. "*Sancta Maria*," he says then. "How am I supposed to follow that? Brother, if you want to know what *bathos* is, you're about to find out. I was going to say, what defines life for me is the autumn song of a robin. So casual and simple and unaffected, just natural; but it always lifts your heart. To me, that's what life is about – I can't express it in words, but I do find it in the song, every time I hear it. *Every* time. It starts such gratitude in my heart."

And then they share with Brother Cyril what they think their last words might be. Brother Cassian says he sincerely hopes he will die in his sleep, with no advance warning and no kerfuffle of any kind. He says he hopes his last words will simply be, “Good night.”

Brother Josephus sits quietly, thinking. “Can I have this?” he asks, then, “Does it count? My namesake is St Joseph of Nazareth, husband of Mary. And you know, one of the intriguing things about St Joseph is that we read quite a bit about him, his dreams, the struggle of his conscience in marrying Mary, his decisive action that saved the life of Jesus as a child, his work as a carpenter, his obedience to the call of God . . . quite a bit. But he never speaks. He manages to convey so much without uttering a single word. I am named for him. I think it would be fitting if I gave my life back to God in the prayer of the heart, the prayer of silence. I think that might be best.”

As he looks at Brother Cyril then, it strikes Cyril how attractively sweet and gentle is his smile. *Another one*, he thinks, *who just is what he is, who doesn’t pretend.*

As he slips back through the door in the wall Brother Josephus left unbolted, and dodges the puddles in the abbey court on the way back to the cloister, he realises how much he enjoyed their company. Getting to know his community one by one feels so intriguing, and so satisfying. *This*, he thinks, *is the best idea I ever had.*

Chapter Sixteen

There might have been a better day for a novice to come across to the infirmary in search of material for his book. Of the infirmary brothers and its residents, the only one left on Brother Cyril's list is the ancient and bed-bound scribe, Brother Denis. He can still be fed and he can drink from a cup held to his lips. So far, by turning him every few hours and keeping him scrupulously clean, they have protected him from bed sores. He no more speaks than does Father Paul, but – in part inspired by the courtesy and respect with which he saw Father William treat the aged precentor – Brother Cyril doesn't want to leave him out of the story.

It's been a pressured day in the infirmary, though. All the usual things and then, despite the desultory activity of the bees at this time of year, Brother Nathaniel managed to incur seven bee stings helping Brother Mark feed them for the winter and put the mouse guards on the hives; and a cow trod on Brother Placidus's foot, at the same time trapping him against the wall of the milking shed. Neither young man has sustained lasting damage, but Nathaniel is delirious and Placidus shaken and bruised. Brother Felix's back is nearly well enough for him to take up life as normal again, maybe tomorrow, but he still needs their time in extra reassurance as he contemplates emerging from the safety of this cocoon, to face being with everyone else in chapel, in the frater, in the scriptorium. And now this afternoon is their prior's day for his routine enema. Even so, Father William is mildly surprised when Brother Michael asks him if he would mind being the one to look after that for him. Brother Christopher is keeping watch over the two young monks recovering from their mishaps, and the infirmarian offers to keep an eye on Felix and absorb Brother Cyril's visit to Brother Denis. Though he doesn't give it much thought, being in the middle of clearing tables and mopping floors when the infirmarian asks him, it lodges somewhere in William's consciousness as odd. He is used to administering enemas now, but it's generally the infirmarian who takes on this responsibility, while William attends to chores more often allocated to a dogsbody than requiring the attention of a physician. Why occupy the infirmarian's time with Brother Cyril, and ask the assistant to take on the more skilled task?

William carries his pail of dirty water out to toss onto the tree roots, and encounters the authorial novice on his way in. "Oh, hello," he says. "You've come to see Brother Denis, haven't you? Brother Michael said. Erm . . . I'm not sure where he is."

As he straightens up and turns away from the tree with the bucket in his hand, he freezes, suddenly completely still, his gaze arrested by something in the orchard; the novice looks to see what has so caught his eye, but nothing seems to be out of place or unusual. Walking slowly down from the kitchen garden in their direction are the prior and the infirmarian, happy and companionable together, completely engrossed in conversation as they stroll along in step, a picture of absolute affection and accord.

Nothing about this strikes Brother Cyril as worthy of note at all, and when Father William suddenly asks him how his book is going and if he's pleased with it so far – a question definitively guaranteed to attract Brother Cyril's attention – he's entirely content to have his focus redirected.

The infirmarian and the prior saunter comfortably through the gap in the wall, joining them under the cherry tree almost bare of leaves but bejewelled with raindrops – looking so cheerful, Brother

Cyril thinks.

"I'll hand you over to William, then," says Brother Michael to Father Francis with a smile, "and I'm at your disposal with our Brother Denis, Brother Cyril." He offers the novice a playfully ceremonial bow, and takes him through into the infirmary.

"I can't recall," remarks William, as he then begins to walk across the garden to the bath house with Father Francis, "ever seeing you and Brother Michael in the same place together before."

"No?" says the prior easily, looking with bland friendliness at William. "In Chapter, surely, and in the Office, or at Mass?"

"Yes," says William. "I meant, talking with him, just the two of you."

"Oh well," says the prior casually, "our paths don't that often cross."

"And you keep it that way?" William asks him.

At these words, the prior stops and steadily meets his eye. "Yes," he says, "we do. We came to an accommodation."

William regards him thoughtfully. "Francis, does our abbot know about this?"

He sees the flash of indignation this incurs, but he waits anyway. "I don't know what you think you mean by 'this,'" says the prior, "but yes, he does. It . . . only twice was there anything we should have confessed to our abbot, and we did so. He knew. Not Abbot John, I mean – Father Peregrine. Look, William, it was all a long time ago. We both wanted not just to stay here, but to . . . er . . . uphold the trust in us implied in our vows. We renounced it and we have stood firm, and yes, John also knows. It maybe isn't as clear-cut as, say, Father John and Rose, or you and Madeleine; the challenges of the situation are different – we live in community together; the temptation to dishonesty is more persistent, perhaps. Though comparisons aren't always helpful; heaven knows, you suffered enough, and so did John, and so – in a different way – did we. Still do, to some extent. Mind you, I don't know why I'm telling you all this because, to be candid, I can't see what business of yours it would be in any case. There is nothing I am ashamed of. Even so, I'll be grateful if you don't talk about it to anyone."

Francis resists the urge to take a step back as he finds himself on the receiving end of William's direct gaze. "Of course I'm not going to talk about it," says William. "What do you take me for?

"I esteem you," he adds. "It cannot have been easy then, or now. And I'm sorry if I was intrusive, Francis. You're right, of course you are – it's not my business. But . . . what can I say . . . consider me an ally. I understand. So, then, everything's ready for you here, Father. If you'd like to visit the reredorter, I'll be in the bath house when you come through."

Checking the heat of the water kettles, adding some small chunks of wood to the fires, looking over the towel waiting on the side and feeling to make sure the herbal tisane in the pitchers is the right temperature, as he waits for Francis to return, William reflects that many of the stories of monasticism remain enfolded in silence. They are not lost, but neither are they told, or enacted, or finished. Their last chapter will never be written; and that, too, is a way of keeping faith. It is recorded in the book of life. He thinks about the integrity and the cost of all the different kinds of love, and he gives thanks for the barefoot tracks left by love walking through his own life, every form of it a manifestation of wonder. Without love, he thinks, there is nothing of humanity but dust.

* * *

Brother Denis's health is declining. Where he used to be able to sit in the little infirmary frater for his meals, and out in the sunshine when the weather is warm, now he just keeps to his room. He's lying on his bed, just resting, but he's not asleep. His eyes are open. As Brother Cyril sits beside the bed on the low stool the infirmarian has put there for him, he isn't quite sure if those eyes see him or not. The old man is very thin and curled up. It occurs to Cyril that he looks completely relaxed and contented. It strikes him that the infirmary brothers must have done a good job, and maybe that Brother Denis himself has done good work too, in forging for himself a soul equal to this long, slow walk through the unclaimed and unwanted wasteland of extreme old age.

He wonders whether to say anything at all about his book, or just reach into the silence to find what he can. Then Brother Michael, sitting on the old man's chair set near the foot of the bed, speaks. "This is Brother Cyril, Brother Denis. He was our postulant only a few weeks ago, now he's one of our novices, and he's already writing a book! Isn't that exciting? Personally, I can't wait to read it, because it has our story in it – ha! Like the Bible! It's all about us. Brother Cyril has a set of questions he's asking each one of us about what we've made of the way of faith. If you don't mind, Brother, since you are in a retreat of holy silence for now, I'm taking the liberty of answering his questions for you. But we thought you might appreciate that happening in your presence. What's his first question, Brother Cyril?"

"I wonder, Brother Denis, what you have learned, in your years as a monk."

Brother Michael waits a moment before responding. "You can see, I think, from Brother Denis's eyes and the tranquillity in his face, that he has learned patience – which is so important for us all. Patience is indispensable in monastic life. You won't get far without it.

"Even with the chattiest brothers, it's not always easy to discern what's happening with them at the soul level. With someone like Brother Denis, who lives in holy silence all of every day, it can be especially difficult to evaluate what he's experiencing, what work he's doing, and how long this stretch of his journey will be. But what we do know – with complete confidence – is that in his own way he will make it through, he will triumph in the end. Even if we can't see the progress he's making now, or determine the nature of it, we can see his patience and his courage in quietly staying here with us. We honour him for it.

We are so grateful to have Brother Denis here in the infirmary."

"Patience, then," says Cyril. "I won't forget. My next question is what Brother Denis would like to achieve."

Even though he's invested in this undertaking, Brother Cyril can't help feeling it sounds a bit pointless. But Brother Michael says, "One of the things we aspire to in monastic life – and talk about; it will certainly come up in your novitiate studies – is holy death. It's a really important objective we don't lose sight of, ever. We travel towards it consciously and intentionally – *memento mori*. We are encouraged to remember that here we have no abiding city, but we look for the one that is to come. We are here for a season on this Earth, but we are turned towards the light of heaven. And our time here is astonishingly short, even though sometimes it feels like it's going on for ever. Brother Denis is now engaged on the greatest work of all – and reminding the rest of us of its importance, too – he is making a holy death. It humbles us that we have the privilege of supporting him as he does so. It's like when Moses prayed through the battle of Amalek, and as long as he held up his hands in prayer the people of God prevailed. But he got tired of standing there with his hands upraised. So Aaron and Hur pulled a big stone over for him to sit on, and they held up his hands for him. The power of God rested on Moses, but it was his brother and his friend who helped him fulfil it. That's what's happening here, as Brother Denis takes on the heroic task of making a holy death. We're holding up his hands for him, so he doesn't fail in his calling."

Brother Cyril can see this is actually true. The infirmarian isn't saying it just to make Brother Denis feel good, or to sound pious. Not only does Brother Michael absolutely believe it, but it is also demonstrably taking place. He has to sit in silence for a moment to let it sink in, and he feels an impulse of gratitude that you can do that here without anyone wondering what's wrong with you. Then he says – by this time with more confidence there may be an honest answer – "And I wanted to know what you feel your life is all about, Brother

Denis."

Brother Michael says, "I think you know Brother Denis was one of our scribes. If you go up to the library – that's assuming you ever get a spare moment, given all you've taken on – I'm sure Father Chad will be able to show you the books Brother Denis wrote out and illuminated for our community. But I'm not sure I'd count that as quite what his life is all about. It was his occupation, and he did it well, but there's more to him than that.

"One of the most frightening and devastating things that can happen to a person is being abandoned, being excluded and bereft, being left alone. As you travel along with us, you'll maybe notice that Father Benedict touches upon that in our Rule, when he speaks about excommunication and exclusion from the common table when a brother has done something seriously wrong. The greatest thing we have, you know, is each other. It's our strength. That someone wants to join our community, as you have just done, Brother Cyril, is the greatest compliment and the dearest joy. And I would say that Brother Denis's life has become all about that most wonderful of things – letting us know, day by day, that we are not alone; in spite of all the struggles age and infirmity have thrown at him, he still elects to stay with us. We are not alone. Truly, what more precious gift could anybody give?"

Brother Cyril listens to this carefully, privately marvelling that Brother Michael can get so much that is honestly valid out of such unpromising material. "So my last question is," he says, "what you would like your last words on this Earth to be."

Again, Brother Michael sits with the question quietly, and then he says, "I am certain you know off by heart, Brother Cyril, the story of the Annunciation. How the angel came to Mary with the invitation to become the mother of God. One of the hallmarks of the presence of Jesus is that even though he is Lord, he doesn't dominate. He doesn't push, he doesn't invade, he doesn't overrule. He treats us with absolute respect. He stands at the door and knocks. So it was when the angel came to Mary. She was asked for her enthusiastic consent, and nothing went forward without it. And so she gave her *fiat*, "Be it unto me according to your word." She gave her Amen – with all the mind-boggling complexity and complications of its consequences. At the end of Brother Denis's life, he will be invited home to glory; the doorway into the presence of Jesus will open for him. When it does, one of us – either our abbot or Father William – will strengthen his soul with the *viaticum*, the food for his journey, and absolve him from every clinging sin that weighs him down. At the end, there'll be the opportunity to say his Amen. And because he is in silence, we will say it for him; not to overrule, but because he trusts us; because he is a brother of this house, and we know his faithfulness, his vocation. We know his heart.

"Is that . . . does that help you?"

"Patience," says Brother Cyril, "and making a holy death. Knowing we are not alone. Responding to the invitation of Christ with our own Amen. Have I got that right, Brother Denis, Brother Michael?"

"You certainly have," says the infirmarian with a smile. "What an excellent listener he proved to be, did he not, Brother Denis?"

The old man on the bed, very slowly – it looks as though this is an effort for him – lifts his bony, blue-veined hand in its shroud of wrinkled skin, and gently pats Brother Cyril's hand resting there on the bed beside him. Cyril beholds this in astonishment. It feels like a blessing, a holy thing you could never ask for or expect to be given.

As he takes his leave of Brother Denis and walks back out into the garden with the infirmarian, Brother Cyril discerns a twinge of regret in the centre of his being, that he will have no good reason to come back here for the time being. His own work is at present mainly in the kitchen, and Brother Denis was the last of the infirmary residents he needed to meet. Of course, he will come here once a month for an enema and a bath, but that's not very often, is it? He realises how vivid an encounter this has been, and how surprisingly much it has meant to him. He really likes these men. St Alcuins, he thinks, is a very special place to be.

Brother Michael smiles at him and thanks him for taking the time and trouble to come over specially to see Brother Denis. "Not many people do," he says, "and you are always welcome. Come back whenever you'd like to. It's nice for our men here to have a visitor, and to enjoy a sense of being properly part of the community."

Brother Cyril promises to return whenever the daily round permits, and tucks this invitation away as a treasure. This is not something he'd ever have anticipated or imagined – that the company of aged and dying men, and their carers, could feel like such a grace.

As he walks slowly back along the cobbled path through the trees, he goes over in his mind again the way Brother Michael expressed the priorities of the old scribe's life, to be sure he doesn't forget. He thinks he has time to go into his cell and write it down while it's still fresh in his mind.

He goes into the cloister and climbs the day stairs to the dorter, lets himself into his cell and sits down to write at the little scribe's desk they allowed him to have. When he's got it all written down to his satisfaction, he sits and reads it through. Then he pauses to reflect on it all. He wonders how much of it was Brother Denis, and how much Brother Michael. When he tries to imagine the work of an infirmarian, he can certainly see that patience would have a prominent place in every passing day; and helping men prepare for a holy death must happen often. But what about feeling bereft, utterly alone? What about finding the courage to say his own quiet "Amen" in response to the daunting call of God upon his life – the complicated and complex consequences, the need of help in seeing it through?

It comes to him that however long a time he lives here, he will never come to an end of the voyage of exploration his book has started off. It seems to be generating as many questions as answers.

* * *

At the conclusion of the Morrow Mass, as the abbot follows Father Bernard bearing the gospel cross down the choir aisle, he catches Father William's eye and slightly jerks his head in an invitation, received and understood, to follow him out to the vestry before going through to Chapter. When he arrives there himself, he thanks his sacristan, and says he will put his chasuble and stole away himself. Father Bernard correctly reads this as the courteous dismissal it is, and he sets off to the chapter house as William comes in to the vestry. "Yes?" says William.

John takes off his stole, kissing the cross embroidered on it, and lays it on the long counter to fold it carefully.

"This is our last chance to finalise the decision on whom to send down to Cambridge to be priested," he says. "We'd planned to send Brother Cedd and Brother Felix, but I'm worried about it. Felix *should* be priested, because of his gifts and abilities, but he's so unstable; and Cedd is young to bear such a responsibility, going with him. But he should be priested too, because of the seniority of his position now he's overseeing the scriptorium. I don't know what to do."

He lays the stole away carefully in the drawer where it belongs, undoes the silken rope round his waist and drops it on the work surface, pulls the chasuble off over his head.

"If I were you," says Father William, "what I might choose to do is send a third man – someone steady – and only send one next year. Obviously, it's a big expense all in one year. Do you have enough money laid by?" He knows perfectly well they do, otherwise he wouldn't have suggested it. He borrows the key from Cormac at least twice a week and spends the evening in the checker going through all the ledgers.

"I think we do," says the abbot thoughtfully, and Father William nods respectfully in encouragement of this assessment. "Who do you think, then? For the third man."

"Well," says Father William, "I think your schoolmaster ought to be priested. I'd send Brother Josephus."

"Then who do we put into the school?" asks the abbot, folding the chasuble with care. "Brother Damian is more than capable but he found it so difficult I don't want to put him back in to it. He'd go with good grace, but he'd be unhappy."

"I might be wrong," says Father William with cautious and intentional humility, "but I do believe that if there's one man overlooked and undervalued in this community, it's probably Brother Germanus. I think he'd be more than able to run your school for a year with Brother Cassian, and if you sent him to be priested when Josephus came back, you'd have a stronger oversight in your school. He's a good gardener, because he's intelligent and sensible, and gardening is important of course, but . . . for heaven's sake . . . if he draws up a plan for us, everyone could do two hours gardening once a week and you're sorted."

The abbot puts the folded chasuble in its drawer, with its rope tucked in beside it. He likes this idea.

"I'm sorry we've overlooked him, if that's what we've done – and undervalued him," he says thoughtfully. "Maybe I should have sent him sooner."

"It's no bad thing," William says swiftly. He hadn't meant to criticise his abbot. "There's nothing like maturity. If you have a young man with real intellect, clearly gifted, and you reward his abilities and promote him to responsibility too early, you can end up with someone capricious and unevenly developed – too little experience of life to evaluate situations shrewdly, too much confidence in his own judgement."

The abbot looks at him sharply. "I hope that's not what I've done with Brother Cedd. I put him there after Father Clement had to stop, because we had no one else who could do it – only Theodore or James, and we need them where they are."

A faint gleam of humour appears in William's face. "Brother Cedd s safeguarded from any kind of hubris by an unshakeable conviction of his own mediocrity," he says. "It's not the same as humility – Father Columba had humility, so does Father Francis, and that's a special quality – but in community it's a workmanlike substitute. He'll be all right. He's too busy thinking about manuscripts to think about himself, these days. Father, shouldn't we go through to Chapter? They'll be waiting for you."

"Yes, I'm sorry," says John. "That's a decision then. I'll put that to them. Three men this year – send Josephus with the other two – and Brother Germanus in the school for this year, then send him to be priested after that. Thanks, friend. I knew you'd know what to do."

Chapter Seventeen

Brother Cyril reads carefully through the list his novice master gav
him, running his finger down the names and bringing to mind th
faces. He stops at Brother Boniface because he can't think whic
monk that even is, let alone where to find him. He traces along t
the list of occupations. Oh. Another scribe. That'll be why he neve
sees him then. He never goes near the scriptorium if he can help it, s
rooted has his aversion become to running the risk of further derisio
from Brother Philip. He wonders how to get to speak to Brothe
Boniface, since the calefactory is off-limits to him until he's taken h
solemn vows. He decides to work out which man Boniface must be, b
observation in chapel and Chapter and at mealtimes, and catch hi
on the way out of one of these occasions when the community come
together. Actually, thinking about it, he must be that tall, thin, dar
young man with the serious face, because who else could it be?

So, after High Mass, he interrupts the flow of brethren leavin
the choir in the direction of the frater, to get alongside him. "Are yo
Brother Boniface?" he asks very quietly (they mustn't chat here).

"Yes," says Boniface, stopping. Brother Cyril sees that his fac
as well as serious, is also friendly, kind. "Can I make a time for m
questions?" he asks him.

"Yes," Boniface says again. "I'll come and find you in the kitche
shall I, when we've eaten?"

While they're washing dishes and wiping down the table an

Brother Conradus is cutting up vegetables to set the soup cooking for suppertime, Brother Boniface appears in the kitchen. Brother Cyril, still with a dish rag in his hand, stops what he's doing and brings two stools over to the fireside for them to sit down. Brother Benedict, coming back from the dairy where he's taken the butter left over from the midday meal, says, "Oh, hello Boniface. Is this about Brother Cyril's book? D'you want my answers as well, Brother Cyril, since I'm here?"

Benedict and Boniface, Brother Cyril discovers, went through the novitiate together and are good friends. Cyril has been meaning to make a time to see Brother Benedict, who works right next to him in the kitchens every day, but there is that oddity of being always with someone – it makes it difficult to identify one particular moment as any more suitable than another.

He enjoys the sense of these men being at ease in each other's company, knowing one another well. Boniface courteously gestures to Benedict to go first, and Benedict says the main thing he's learned is to be adaptable – that things you found daunting and thought you'd hate doing often turn out to be interesting and easier than they looked. Boniface says something really important he's learned is to take nothing for granted; to check, and then check again. If you've done the illuminated capital on a page, and already gilded it, and then you make a stupid spelling mistake there's no room to correct, or miss out a word, it makes you wish you were dead. Likewise if you assume someone has it in for you and is doing something on purpose, but you don't make time to talk to them, it generates all kinds of ill feeling. Just check. Ask. Listen. Look. Think.

Benedict says the achievement he wants to work on is – seriously – staying awake. He has this awful habit of nodding off in chapel, and he needs to figure out how to overcome it, because he knows it's irreverent and he finds it so embarrassing. Boniface smiles and nods in sympathetic agreement. He says his primary ambition this year is to deepen his practice of prayer; not so much in the Office or at Mass, but his private, personal prayer. He has the sense that it bores him because he's essentially shallow, and he needs to address that. He says that their founding fathers' edict, *ora et labora*, might be his way in; if he can start by making the silence and focus of the scriptorium a doorway into contemplation – perhaps that could become, for him, what his life is about. But knows he's not there yet, not by a country mile.

Benedict says, for him, life is about intentional community. He can no longer imagine life as a householder, as a tradesman, or as a merchant. He respects that we each have our own calling, but he finds such riches of soul in the common life of the monastic way. It is that above all else he can feel shaping his life. He says he can't really think what his last words might be, but that he knows the desire of his heart is to stay close to his Lord. Blushing slightly, because this strikes deep, feels very personal, he says that as he sets out on the momentous journey from everything he has known and loved here, he might want to say simply, "Please, don't let go of my hand."

Brother Cyril glances at Brother Boniface's expression, listening to this, and loves the gentleness and understanding he sees there. Boniface waits, allows some space for Benedict's words to settle and be received, before he says, "Sometimes I think – with reference to what I want my life to be about – that the best picture of it is if you could imagine a man just quietly breathing . . . in . . . out . . . absorbing some things . . . letting others go . . . becoming more open . . . but also learning to be enfolded into silence and retreat, withdraw like a snail into its shell. It has a kind of paradox, or a counterpoint, or something, a rhythm of opposites. And my last words? I've given your question a lot of thought, and I think if I could choose, I'd like to finish my life with a specific request to be taken into the Sacred Heart of Jesus, and make that my dwelling place."

Benedict, very quietly, says, "Amen."

* * *

Brother Cyril has spoken to just about everyone. He still has to see his abbot – he feels distinctly nervous about that, and does what he can to put it out of his mind – but there is also the novice master, and his fellow novices.

He has generated a huge amount of notes, and spent ages every evening carefully writing up whatever he has gleaned from conversations in the course of the day. Conscious of the expectation that he will be frugal with his use of the paper from Norfolk and the ink, he's penned his notes in the smallest, close, crabbed script. He hasn't written in the margins because he didn't leave any. He began right at the top and wrote to the very edges of each page. He's worn out three quill pens and had to go back time and again to the checker, to humbly beg permission of the cellarer to take yet more sheets from the store.

"Look," said Brother Cormac in the end, "just take two dozen sheets, why don't you? I've sent for some more, anyway, and you can always bring them back if you don't use them. Beg an extra jar of ink from Brother Walafrid if you need it. Tell him I said you could. Or at least fill your ink horn from a jar in the scriptorium – and while you're there, pick up a spare pen from Brother Cedd, they've got loads. If you've got permission to write this thing, you might as well do it properly. That's what the materials are for."

Grateful and excited, he did exactly that. And now his book is almost done. It hasn't taken as long as he thought it would, they're only just coming up to Martinmas tomorrow; it all took shape with astonishing speed because he got so wrapped up in it, though he still has to render it into a fair hand, of course. He feels confident that he has represented faithfully everything confided to him; he's just not quite certain about his spelling. Father Theodore told him it wouldn't be necessary to translate it all into Latin, which came as a relief.

The shape of the monastic day changed into its winter form at Michaelmas, and since October they have begun to light a small fire on the hearth for their morning studies in the novitiate schoolroom. It blows back a little on this blustery morning with the wind coming from the east, off the moor, but even though the room's slightly smoky as they gather in their study circle, they're glad of the warmth.

They hear Father Theodore coming up the stairs from Chapter. He closes the door behind him as he walks into the room to take his place in the ring of low benches and stools.

They've been familiarising themselves with the great early saints of the church, the desert fathers in their caves, the founders of Christian monasticism, but the novice master says they're going to take a break from that this morning, and reflect together on the questions Brother Cyril has given them, for his book. He says he feels sure they will have read them carefully, now they've had plenty of time to reflect on them, and he wonders if they would like to respond all together. "Will that be all right for you, Brother Cyril?" he asks. "Is it unfair of me to expect you to remember what everybody says?" But Cyril feels hopeful that he can manage, and promises to check with everyone before his manuscript is given to the novice master and the abbot for their approval.

Brother Cyril simply cannot evaluate which is worse; his disappointment over the reduction of his name in monasticism to a permanent joke, or his disappointment at the conversation that now ensues.

It begins with Brother Philip, quick to jump in with the observation that anything he personally learns just seems to go in one ear and out of the other. He feels he's learned a huge amount about what to do when – how to pronounce infernally difficult names in the Bible, how to keep up with finding his way round the breviary, how to extinguish a candle without splashing any wax, how to ask someone to pass the salt without speaking – but the really important stuff, doctrine and finer points of theology, he finds hard to retain.

There is an immediate chorus of agreement, with examples coming thick and fast of things people have learned like washing their hands before meals, not letting the incense smother the charcoal in the thurible, the right form of words to beg someone's pardon, where Brother Cedd keeps the recipe book for inks – aye, and where to find a ball of string – memorising the Latin grace for the end of the meal (the abbot says the one at the beginning). There's a lot of laughter and agreement that there is altogether so much to learn it makes their head spin – who could ever have imagined the simple life of monasticism could be so spectacularly complicated?

It's Philip again who bores of this first and segues into consideration of what he would like to achieve. He says that though obviously he'd love to be canonised some day, as things stand right now he'd settle not even for actually *staying awake* through the reading of the martyrology but just managing to doze off discreetly, skipping the sudden loud snort and jerk of his lolling head that usually gives him away. His graphic pantomime of this all too familiar event is greeted with a gale of laughter from Brother Anthony and Brother Nathaniel. Anthony says all he wants to be able to achieve at the moment is walking up the day stairs carrying an armful of books without catching his foot in the hem of his tunic. Philip and Nathaniel both laugh, and Nathaniel says *amen*, and that he personally is nursing an ambition to spend even one morning weeding without getting the skirts of his habit all clarted up with cleavers – spring and summer – or burrs now it's autumn. It takes him forever to pick them all off, and he ends up scurrying late into chapel.

So having done their best with what they'd like to achieve, Philip leads the charge into an examination of what their lives are all about. Mostly, he says, with a dramatic pause between each word, he has . . . absolutely . . . no . . . idea . . . whatsoever. In fact, he's kept so fully occupied with running here and there and getting everything right, he's torn between wasting no time on even asking, or concluding, that the tearing around has become what his life now *is* all about.

Brother Anthony says his life – especially on fast days – sometimes threatens to deteriorate into being all about the next meal. Planting and pruning and tilling the earth, he works up such an appetite he could eat a roast suckling pig all by himself some days, and though there's no denying Brother Conradus bakes a loaf to set before a king, there's a limit to how far an egg and a piece of fruit and a handful of salad will take you.

Brother Nathaniel nods vigorously – evidently that's territory he knows all too well – but says *his* life has mostly been about clattering up and down the farm track trying to get the harvest in and threshed and winnowed before the storms break, but at the same time walking in to the church before the abbot has given the knock for prayers to begin. Up and down that track, up and down, yes, that builds up a mighty hunger too, he agrees.

Brother Philip has one of Cyril's small slips of parchment in his hand. He's half-listening to Brother Nathaniel, but wants to move on to a consideration of what his last words on Earth might be. He suggests that if you were dying, you might be past speaking at all, or your death might be sudden and give you no warning. He wonders aloud about possible eventualities leading to abrupt and unexpected demise – "falling from a ladder, mending a roof, thatching a rick slipping on icy steps, being kicked by a horse, tripping on an uneven flag on the floor and falling into the fire". Nathaniel's got a few of hi own – "getting lockjaw from a rose thorn, being struck by lightning".

"Or what about being gored by a bull? Or a loose slate falling from the roof you mended, splitting your skull open?" Brother Anton interrupts him.

Sitting listening to this unfolding around him, Brother Cyril has an awful sense of losing his grip on the dignity of being Brother Anybody sliding ignominiously back into being just Rufus O'Conaill, a lad who with every passing minute, is getting more and more perilously near to tears. The one thing he hopes, quite desperately, as he clenches his teeth tight together and stares across the circle into the low-burning fire, is that Father Theodore won't ask him a question, won't make him try to speak. He knows he could not.

"I've never told you about my novice master." Theodore's quiet voice cuts across the lively conversation, and they fall silent, attending to what he has to say. It sounds intriguing. "I don't normally speak about him, because we didn't have an easy relationship. One of the things I've been *taught* is that if you can't say something good about a person then you should say nothing about them at all. But something I've *learned* is that there occasionally comes a right time to tell your story, even if it doesn't make other people look good.

"My novice master – his name was Father Matthew – schooled us diligently in Latin and Greek and Hebrew; rehearsed us in doctrine and church law and the Benedictine Rule; made sure we knew all about the saints; punctiliously taught us theology. He was a good man, and assiduous in carrying out his duty to oversee our formation. Something he was very fond of repeating, a maxim he'd learned from a bishop, he said, to help us understand that we were to be malleable, teachable and humbly receptive, was, 'Nobody cares what you think.' He said it to us as a group, and also as individuals. He wanted to make quite certain we understood that our conversion, sanctification and formation came from the dogma and tradition of holy Church; we were not to dilute or pollute it with our own wayward thoughts. 'Nobody cares what you think.'

"But even if no one cared, I *did* think about that, quite a lot. More disturbingly, I found I disagreed. I still do disagree. I care very much about what you think, and I always want to hear it. I feel it as such an honour when you come to share the thoughts of your heart with me. Something I would most dearly love to achieve, is to see the men who as novices come under my care, develop the confidence and grounding to think for themselves – to be able not only to soak up the teaching we already have, but bring their own insights and contribution to the witness of faith.

"I've listened carefully this morning to what's been said in our circle, and it reminded me powerfully of how muddled and tired and out of my depth I felt in my own novitiate year – trying to get everything right, to arrive where I should be – crucially, at the right time. Mostly I got it wrong, and in the end I lost all hope and all confidence. I got beyond discouragement and became entirely desolate. I ended up sobbing on our abbot's floor – Father Peregrine back then, not Father John – and he put me back together. He cared about me. He wanted to understand. In order to understand someone, you have to know their story. I clung to his kindness and understanding like a drowning man lost from a shipwreck clinging to a rock. Because of him, I realised that I wanted my life to be about helping the men who come to try their vocation here feel that they are worth something, feel respected and loved and encouraged.

"And, in case you were wondering, I'd like my last words on Earth to be a prayer I learned from a beautiful priest of God: 'Abba, I belong to you.'

"So, as I sat here with a sudden vivid recall of Father Matthew telling me, 'Nobody cares what you think,' I wanted to make sure you know that I do care immensely, both about what you think and what you feel; and I hope you can trust me enough to always tell me, if you want to. Whatever it is, whatever your concerns may be, however private and personal they might feel. We are all human. But, Brother Ignatius, we haven't heard from you. You've sat here very quietly while the others were chatting. What did you make of Brother Cyril's questions?"

The quiet flow of what he said to them has made enough of a fire break between the hilarious tossing about of Cyril's ideas and the present moment, created a safe space to receive a serious response. Brother Cyril, who still can't look at anyone, braces himself in case his questions are even further mocked and dismissed. He knows he can't get up and leave the room – how would he ever come back? He knows he has nothing in him to withstand any further corrosion of trivialising laughter. What is he, after all, but Cyril the Squirrel, a figure of fun?

"Well," says Brother Ignatius, cautiously, "yes. I have been thinking about these questions every day, actually. I know Brother Cyril's been talking with the brothers in full profession throughout the whole community, and I have to admit I am just agog – I simply cannot wait to read what they said. I have so many questions myself, like, how many people said the same thing or were they all different? How much of what they say has come from exploring what is unresolved inside them? What has come from the example of other people? Oh, so many things I'm curious to find out.

"Like everyone else here, I'm learning a lot very fast, of course. So, yes, as others have said, it takes some reflection to identify what my *soul* is learning, if you see what I mean, as distinct from picking up everything I need to know to find my way round. I think I can identify one massive big lesson I've learned here. I don't know that it's terribly deep, but I do think it's important: everyone needs a friend. Just that. If you have no friend in the world, you're sunk. Everyone needs a friend.

"What I'd like to achieve, apart from just getting through and the community being willing to allow me to make my simple vows, is something I see everywhere and I hugely admire. There's a kindness in men's eyes, here. As much as that fire is glowing, their kindness shines. I can see it, like a steady, quiet light. I cannot tell you how much I want that for myself. If one day that kindness shines from my face, my eyes, too, then my work here is done.

"What I want my life to be about is . . . erm . . . you know, like when Brother Germanus espaliers a pear tree onto a pergola? I want my whole life to be conformed upon the beauty of our Rule, because I love it. I wish I'd known St Benedict, I really do. I want my life to be the lungs that his Rule breathes through, a heart that the blood of his Rule pumps through.

"And when my day on Earth is done, I want my last words to be what we say at Compline: 'May the Lord almighty grant us a quiet night and a perfect end. Into thy hands, O Lord, I commend my spirit. Thou hast redeemed us, Lord, thou God of truth.' Even *if* I get kicked by a horse or fall down some icy steps, that's still the last thing that I'd like to go through my mind."

Exactly as he finishes saying these words, the chapel bell begins to ring the Angelus. It's time for the midday Office. Father Theodore looks at Brother Ignatius and thanks him, then turns to glance at the fire, to check it is safe to leave. After that he dismisses the circle of novices, with a smile and a small bow of courtesy to them. They stand, in the respect due to him as their novice master. He goes first to the door, and holds it open as they come through; but, "Brother Philip," he says as they begin to leave. Philip stops on his way out to see what the novice master wants of him, and Theodore falls in beside him, to walk along the upper passage of the cloister and down the day stairs. Brother Cyril, walking just in front of them with the others, in the silence expected of them, hears Father Theodore say in his usual friendly tone, "Thank you so much for your contribution to our discussion today. I'm really sorry to give you so little chance to disarrange whatever you already have in place, but please would you, of your charity, come back after the midday meal? There's something I need to talk to you about."

"Oh," says Philip, surprised, "all right. Will it take long? Because I'm supposed to be helping Father Gilbert with some stacks of music that need putting back into order."

Brother Cyril isn't totally certain, but he has an idea that asking the novice master if what he has in mind will take long might not be best monastic practice – for a novice.

Father Theodore doesn't instantly reply, but when they are halfway down the stairs, he says, "Um . . . I can't be entirely sure. It depends how our conversation unfolds. But I have a feeling it may be longer rather than shorter. Don't worry about Father Gilbert. I'll have a word with him after Mass, before we go into the frater. You just concentrate on coming back upstairs to see me. But, thank you for your sense of responsibility towards him."

And then they are filtering through from the north range into the south transept of the church, and all conversation must cease. Brother Ignatius, walking beside Brother Cyril, risks a glance at him, and very slightly raises his eyebrows. Otherwise his face remains entirely neutral. *That's something else you've learned, then*, thinks Cyril. You could, he muses, devote a whole text exclusively to the communicatory use of eyebrows in monastic silence.

Chapter Eighteen

The abbot sits at his table, thinking, very still. His hands are round the edges of the manuscript pages on the table in front of him, but he's gazing into space, turning over in his mind the not very easy conversation he's just had with Father Theodore, Brother Michael and Father William – about Brother Felix.

He has a sense of uncertainty about the whole situation. He wonders if they should never have professed that young man in the first place. Is he too fragile, too obsessive, not sufficiently at peace with himself for this way of life? He agrees with the others that Father Gilbert is not the right confessor for him, but feels queasy about Michael's and Theodore's recommendation that Felix be allocated to Father William. God alone knows where that might lead. William is not the most predictable of men; and yet, he found his way to Felix's trouble when no one else had, didn't he? Felix . . . A man who agonises obsessively about one thing will only find a different peg to hang his anguish on if you remove the first one, in John's experience. He hopes the work on his liver with herbs and enemas will gradually bring out old poisons that got into him somehow, and let peace reassert itself.

The community has ratified the decision to send Felix to university to be priested, this next time round. Josephus will go with him as well as Brother Cedd, but was it wise to go ahead? Is it prudent, is it even responsible? On the other hand, if they withdraw the opportunity, that will signal clearly a lack of trust, a disappointment. For a young man like him, that would be crushing. When John said in the Chapter meeting that there had been a change of plan, he had seen Felix steel himself against humiliation, expecting to hear that he would not be going to Cambridge this year, after all. When he heard that the change was the addition of an extra man, to give some support as he hadn't been well, he was so relieved it brought him to the edge of tears. The abbot could see it.

Father John runs through it all one more time in his mind. It's right, he thinks, but risky. He knows beyond doubting the solid power of prayer – and one thing's for sure, they're going to need it this time.

He brings his attention back to the commitments of the afternoon, and looks down at the manuscript he's holding. Paper. Why? When he signed off on two orders for paper from Norfolk, he assumed it was for wrapping powders or something – not for writing on. It's too absorbent really, the letters blur a little, but yes, it suffices. Oh. This is Cormac, isn't it? Paper. From plants, not animals. Well, the fair copy will be written up on parchment, or vellum if they've got enough, whatever Cormac thinks. It's not a huge book, and there won't be lots of illuminations taking up space. There'll probably be enough vellum, and that will signal to Brother Cyril that his abbot honours this work.

He is intrigued by what he's read; it's interesting. He feels he knows his community better than he did before, and some of it was unexpected; not obvious, maybe. Illuminating. The lad has a way of condensing into appropriate written form what John knows all too well will have been a rambling and approximate original discourse. He wonders how the aptitude will develop.

Something's tugging at the abbot's mind, distracting him. Felix, still Felix. But he needs to set that to one side. So he stops; he very consciously and deliberately takes Felix and his problems, and wraps them up, enfolds them completely in prayer like the softest, whitest laundered linen. He takes the whole bundle of it reverently in the hands of his soul, and places it into the cupped hands of Jesus, stretched out to him to receive it. In the inner chamber of his mind, he watches his Lord close his own scarred hands protectively around the whole thing, and lift it away. Now he can give his attention to Brother Cyril. Just as well, he thinks, as the knock comes at the door.

* * *

This feels like such a luxury. Outside on this late November day it's cold and starting to rain, and up in the novitiate they're working on New Testament Greek at present, which is difficult and takes concentration. Normally he wouldn't be allowed to do anything except his novitiate studies in the morning, but if the abbot asks to see you, that's different. Here he is, by some wondrous miracle, sitting in a chair right next to a lovely warm fire, being offered a cup of ale and a honey cake by Brother Thomas, invited to talk with his abbot about his book.

Only the day before yesterday he brought his manuscript for Father John to approve, and the abbot says he's read the whole thing through and is ready to discuss it. The only part lacking before it's completed and bound – subject to the approval that he hopes will be forthcoming today – is the abbot's own response to the four questions.

Looking at Father John sitting opposite him in the firelight and dim shadows of the back end of the year, he thinks how much he loves the sense of this man's presence. There's a warmth, an honesty. This is someone he can trust. You don't find such men often. Not in a whole lifetime maybe. With that, though, he can't help noticing his abbot looks somehow . . . maybe "tired" is the right word . . . this morning. Brother Cyril really hopes he personally is not a burden to bear, that his book is not an imposition or one more thing on an interminable list of matters requiring attention. He hopes with all his heart it can be better than that.

"Did you think, when you came here," his abbot asks, "that you'd be writing a book?"

"No," says Cyril, decisively. "It was Brother Ignatius who thought of it, not me. I never thought of myself as a writer – and I don't now, either. It just sort of happened."

The abbot smiles. "Yes. I know what you mean. It never crossed my mind that I'd be the abbot either. What life asks of us, places into our hands to do, is unexpected, feels laughably impossible, and yet, somehow, we recognise as being our own. It becomes our work, it draws down from our hearts. Somehow, we become the work."

Brother Cyril looks at him, surprised. "Yes," he says. "Yes. That's exactly what it feels like."

"So . . ." Abbot John turns his head and looks into the fire glowing on the hearth. "Did you . . . shall I tell you the answers I had, to the questions you asked?"

This also surprises Cyril. He imagined, when Abbot John invited him to come to his house, a man conscious of his authority and position, delivering with confidence an abbot's message to the community, fulfilling this endeavour with a superior's wisdom. What he had not expected was someone who speaks with simplicity, who evidently thinks of himself as no more than a man like any other, who knows his own mind but doesn't see himself as particularly important. How do you hold on to that, Cyril wonders, when everyone has to stand up if you enter the room, when you hold the power to appoint or to excommunicate, when the whole community listens to your Chapter address every morning, when the cellarer can't send for even a packet of fifty horseshoe nails without your seal and signature on the order? And that puzzlement is laid to rest when he hears what his abbot has to say.

"What I've learned is to lean on Jesus. To turn to him. To grab hold of a fold of his cloak and hold on tight, so I don't lose him in the crowd. Like a little child afraid of losing sight of his mother on market day, I have been afraid to lose sight of Jesus – to be separated, to let go of him. My whole world would end. Without him, I am nothing.

He is there behind my every hope and endeavour. The steady flow of his strength and peace, the light of his countenance . . . this . . . there's no point in my asking what I'd do without him, because I can't even imagine what that could possibly mean. In everything I do – and I cannot begin to tell you, Brother, how often I am completely out of my depth – I turn to him, I turn to him, I turn to him. That's what I've learned to do. It never fails.

"You asked us what we want to achieve." The abbot falls silent, then. Brother Cyril looks at him, his hands clasped loosely, his gaze far away, resting on the fire beyond the flames.

"Only one thing, I think. I want to not let this community down. As Christ has never failed me, so I want to stand firm, to be here for you – for this family of brothers, for all the people who come to us because they need our help. I want it to be a stream that never runs dry. Kindness, where that is needed, straight talking sometimes. A listening ear. Wise heads working out a way forward together. Deciding what to start, what to continue, what to pause, what to stop. Faithfulness in prayer. Ministry of the word and the holy sacrament. And just, I suppose, the gift of my heart. The promise that I will not withhold myself, that we are in this together. I hope, by God's grace, I will never let you down."

Brother Cyril fervently hopes he can remember as much as possible of all this. The community will want to read what their abbot has to say. He must get this committed to memory, get it right.

"What my life is about?" As the abbot looks into the fire, Brother Cyril thinks there is something ageless about him. Yes, he has that firm and decisive quality of maturity, he's not hesitant or unsure, he does have the confidence thoughtfulness requires; and yet he has a humility Cyril normally associates with youth – he really does see himself as nothing special.

"I suppose," the abbot says, "there's a sense in which my life is about less and less. It's the opposite of accretion and accumulation, it's a daily release, a journey into holy poverty. What John the Baptist said, 'He must increase and I must decrease.' I am named for John the Baptist, you know, not John the Evangelist. I think sometimes of the words of Jesus to my namesake, 'Blessed is the man who never loses faith in me.' Heheh. Actually, I believe it means, 'Blessed is the man who doesn't trip over me,' which always makes me smile. I think of it as Jesus sitting in one of our stalls in choir, and me tripping over his foot as I go by. I'm sure he'd put out his hand to steady me. Well, I do – stumble – and he always does reach out to catch me."

He smiles, thinking. Then he sits up straight and looks at Cyril. "That's almost it, isn't it? Oh – except you wanted to know what our last words might be. All I could think of was stupid things like 'Put the cat out' and 'Have you fastened the door of the hen house?' and 'Did you put the butter away in the well?' Besides, our patient community will have sat through so many of my Chapter addresses by the time I'm done, I doubt they will ever want to hear another word from me. But there is one thing. In the years I worked in the infirmary, time and again as men came to the door of death, they told me they could see someone in the room – sometimes a friend, sometimes an angel, it might be someone from their family, or in some cases the Lord himself – at times they even tried to get up and go to greet whoever was there that I couldn't see. It was that vivid for them. The afterlife is a mystery to us, but it seems we do meet again."

He stops. Then he says. "It's not just in dying, though. I've heard tell they are there around us when we come into this world, too. My mother, my sister, they witnessed the birth of many children. They said it was so. It seems the ones who are tasked with watching over us drop us off safely here. I have an idea they travel alongside us, too, if we can develop the sensitivity to recognise it. Then they come to make sure we get safely home. It would be an honour beyond imagining if I could be one of those who comes back to open the way for my brothers – for you, maybe – at the end.

"So, I suppose I might just say, 'See you later,' and that would b
true. Life is so short. And we meet again. Nothing is lost. Everything i
gathered in. What Jesus said, 'Gather up the fragments left over.' Som
of those fragments are ourselves, or parts of ourselves that got lost
trust, innocence, hope, whatever. He . . . he reconciles it all. That's th
work of the cross."

He looks at Cyril. "But, whatever happens at the end or after w
die, let's maybe not get ahead of ourselves. This much I can promis
you: while I'm here, and you're here in this community, I will trave
with you. Please come to me whenever you need to. Please trust me,
you can. Tell me if you are troubled. Please. I am here for you. That's i
I think. That's me. Except . . . about the last words part . . . you knov
if I could die in November or February, I'd like that. If I could see th
glorious flaming dawn you get at those times of year, just once mor
One last look, you know? And now I think that's quite enough abou
me – what about you? Is there anything you wanted to say?"

Sitting there in the fire's warmth and light on this brooding da
looking at his abbot, Brother Cyril thinks what he would really lik
right now, is to tell this man he loves him; but how gushing an
inappropriate would that be? So he just settles for saying he will brin
his notes back to be checked, and respectfully asking if the abbot i
happy with the rest of his book.

Father John smiles. "Oh, yes," he says. "I certainly am. And you'
be writing it up on vellum, yes? Please, not paper. Who's going to bin
it for you, when it's all in a fair hand?"

Brother Cyril affirms that Brother Cedd has given him the vellur
and explains that Father James has volunteered to bind it, and Fathe
Theodore has offered to add in some decorative capitals, one for eac
section.

"You do know," says Abbot John, "Father Theodore's work i
exquisite? It'll be a thing of beauty, you can rest assured.

"I love what you've written. It's splendid. But look, we missed ou time together, to talk through your vocation – well, I did. I forgot. Was there anything more? Anything other than this, that's been on your mind? Anything at all you wanted to talk through?"

Not expecting this question, Cyril has not prepared himself to answer. He feels fairly certain he'll think of something as soon as he leaves, but nothing comes to mind. Then, floating up like a bubble in water from deep inside him, a concern. "Father, I . . . there is only one thing. What if . . . I mean, it's become clear to me, both in what Father Theodore has taught us and in the conversations I've had with the community, that brotherhood and kindness – forbearance, charity, understanding – these are at the heart of our life together. What if . . . what if there's someone I really don't like? Someone who just ruffles my feathers, so to speak. If I have an aversion to someone. What should I do?"

Father John's eyes meet his. Cyril sees the merriment kindled in them, and the abbot laughs. "Familiar!" he says. "It's true for almost all of us, I should think." He pauses, turning the question over in his mind. Then, "I don't want to say anything glib," he says, "because these things are real and can send down roots like dandelions. It's important to be patient with yourself, and – of course – always do your best to be kind. But I would say this. We rub shoulders very close together here. We have our cells, but in community we are very exposed. In truth, it affords us very little privacy beyond what we give one another, and we are required to be honest and open, and to humble ourselves. This life does ask a lot of us; everything we have to give, at times. What I have personally found is that, whoever it is you can't stand, and I'm not going to ask, at some point you'll see him break, see him weep; and then you'll feel differently about him. I don't know how useful that is, but we walk with Christ; such things have a way of finding resolution."

The novice absorbs this, and tucks it away to consider later. He has nothing more to ask. Their conversation is at an end, and Father John walks with him to the way out into the cloister. "Brother Cyril," he says, lifting the latch and opening the oak door, "why did you write your notes on paper? Was it just to save on parchment?"

"Oh – no," says Cyril. "Brother Cormac suggested I might. He thinks, you know, that one day we will write almost everything on paper. He says in some parts of the world they make paper from reeds and write everything on it! Actually, he said parchment and vellum are barbaric and we ought to know better. He said, just try and see how it goes with the paper, for notes at least. And you know, I found it surprisingly easy. I thought the pen would catch and plough it up, but no, it laid down the ink perfectly well. It runs just the tiniest bit, but not enough to make it hard to read."

"Cormac . . ." says the abbot thoughtfully. "Yes, I did wonder. Well, thank you very much, Brother. You've done a fine job."

* * *

The cloud bank has intensified and rain is coming down persistently. Brother Cyril is worried now. What should he do about his habit? It's going to be soaking wet. He'll have to drape it somewhere to dry out – where? – and then either change into his night habit, which means he could end up making his bed damp, and mattresses take forever to dry out, or risk the spare habit in his clothes chest getting as wet as this one later in the day. Not only that, but he feels positive they aren't supposed to be here, in the birch grove by the river at the back of the abbot's house. Nobody ever comes here, it's Father John's private space, Brother Peter told him so. What if Father Abbot comes out of his house? What if they get into trouble? And he has no idea why Brother Philip insisted on going for a walk with him in the pouring rain in the first place. Why would anyone . . .? He wanted to refuse. The last thing on Earth he could imagine choosing to do is go for a walk with Brother Philip, by himself, on even the balmiest summer day. But he could see no way out of it. Their relationship is already uneasy, and having been asked rather bluntly to do this, he couldn't immediately think of a way to say no without the distance between them deepening into actual antagonism and naked dislike. So he said yes, and now here he is, and he wishes he wasn't.

But then he zones back in to what Philip is telling him, walking along plucking narrow leaves off that twig in his hands; something about Father Theodore. "What he actually said to me," Brother Philip is saying, and in his tone of voice Brother Cyril feels puzzled to detect something vulnerable, and a considerable degree of courage, "is that if I wanted to stay in this community another five minutes I'd better go down on my knees to you and beg your forgiveness. And I do, I suppose. I mean, I can't think where else I could go or what else I could do. There haven't been that many court jesters hailed from Helmsley, have there? So . . . I guess . . ."

Brother Cyril feels an intensity that reminds him more than anything else of terror as Brother Philip, the undisputed wit supreme of the novitiate, turns resolutely to block his path and kneels humbly in the wet leaves in front of him. In the form of words he's learned but never used before, Philip says, "I confess to you, my brother, and to God, my sin of thoughtlessness and unkindness, of cruel mockery and stupid, inappropriate levity." He has been assisted in pinpointing these moral errors by what Father Theodore said to him. "And I ask God's forgiveness, and yours." Then he adds, as the novice master forcefully suggested he might, an observation of his own. "I can see I've spoiled something beautiful, and torn down something I'm not capable of putting back. I'm so sorry. Please forgive me. I'm so sorry."

Brother Cyril feels actually sick, under the pressure of this unexpected and intimate personal encounter. He has no idea how this has suddenly happened to him, without any kind of warning whatsoever. The monastic way, well, it might be full of surprises, but not many as huge as this, surely? And now, to cap it all, his head's in such a whirl that he can't remember the form of words for absolution.

And their novice master has impressed upon them, "For mercy's sake, if your brother begs your forgiveness, come through with it quick. It takes him down so low. Any man who kneels before you needs your help."

So he pulls himself together to say, "No, it's all right. I mean, God forgives you, Brother, and so do I. It . . . look . . . let's just start again."

He reaches out his hand, wet with rain, to help Philip get back up on his feet. Now it's become clear why he chose this off-limits location, probably the only place in the abbey where privacy is (almost) assured.

"Just a minute," says Philip, digging in his pocket for his already damp handkerchief, to blow his nose and wipe away what Cyril assumes is rain from his face. "Oh, heaven, these habits are going to be sodden for ever now, aren't they? I'm sorry. You could have stayed in the dry. I know you didn't want to . . . oh . . . damn it. What can I do that's right?"

"Shall we maybe go back indoors?" Brother Cyril suggests diffidently.

"*Yes,*" says Philip. "I've got to look presentable. My father's coming to see me this afternoon. I just needed to get this out of the way first. One nightmare at a time, you know?"

"You . . . aren't you looking forward to seeing your dad?" Cyril asks him in surprise, and Philip laughs.

"What I said, one thing at a time," he says. "That's a story of its own. I'll tell you about that another day." And then, though the rain is coming down hard now and Cyril is feeling distinctly impatient to take cover, Philip stops and it seems only courteous to stop as well, to see why.

"Look," says Philip, "I'm realistic about this; I'm not holding out too much hope. Is there any chance, after all this, that we really could start again, like you said? What I mean is, could we be friends?"

Cyril looks at him, his habit almost soaked by this time, his hair around the tonsure plastered to his head, rain streaming down his entire face – and knows that Philip, looking at him, is seeing the self-same thing. He knows that what he says now will make a lot of difference. If he acquiesces to this request, for one thing, it will leave the responsibility for processing all the disappointment and hurt squarely with himself, while Philip just walks away feeling relieved.

His questions flash through his mind as fast as lightning – what he's learned, what he wants to achieve, what his life is about – and what his last words will be.

"Yes, of course," he says.

Chapter Nineteen

In this year of our Lord 1325, I, Brother Cyril O'Conaill of St Alcuins Abbey in the North Riding of Yorkshire, set out here, in my own words, how the questions I have asked others spoke in turn into my own heart.

First, I asked of them what might they have learned in their years of monastic life.

I have but barely taken up this holy way myself. I am no more than a novice. Hardly may I venture to say I have learned anything worth the writing down.

Even so let me say, as my brothers have of their courtesy and in humility talked with me, their honesty has moved me. They have let me look into their hearts. They have shared with me the lessons of their lives, and may I not in my turn learn from them? If I have learned nothing else, yet have I learned this: to walk with them is an honour, to stay under their roof is a grace, to converse with them is tutelage of itself.

And then I had the temerity to ask, as if they had so far accomplished nothing worthy of record, what thing in this life they desired to achieve? And what have I found but riches that humbled me, and modest, quiet men whose hearts are set upon the way of Christ?

Following along in the track their feet have made, I set down this day that what I, Brother Cyril, long to achieve, is to continue their friend and companion to my life's end. To be worthy of them, and to be worthy of Christ my Master.

After that I laid before them the challenge of telling what their life might in its entirety be about. They spoke of encouragement, of companionship, of faithfulness, of being made whole, of ending histories of hurt, of trust in God, of conformation to St Benedict's holy Rule.

And for me? I, Brother Cyril, aver that my life is about something I have caught sight of in my brothers, and especially in our Abbot John, which is the acquired skill of bringing my undivided attention, a single heart, a quiet eye, my first love, to the way I live. This, I have grasped, is what it means to live in simplicity – what chastity and poverty and obedience and stability *are*, what the very word "monastic" means.

And the last, I importuned them to say to me what they imagined might be their final words upon this Earth, when came the time to return the holy breath of God in them to their Creator. And they spoke of gratitude and thanksgiving, of coming home at the day's end, of joy in a task completed, of encouragement to those left behind, of a reminder to works of charity, of submission to God's goodness in perfect trust.

And in God's name I beseech the Lord Christ that my own last words on Earth might be – learning from him but not, I trust, stealing from him – what my novice master Father Theodore said he hoped would be the last thing he uttered: "Abba, I belong to thee."

Then I offer this book to my abbot in all humility, thanking Father Theodore who painted the capitals for me with such richness and grace, and Father James who has bound it for me with the consummate skill of his hands. May it be, to all who open it, a book of life and hope. May it call you to faith in the goodness of those who walk beside you. For just as they are here, so they also are with you, and in Christ's name they call you on. Take up your way with us, and may your path be blessed.

It started as an endeavour to prove myself, to do something worthwhile; but it became, in the end, for me, a book of gratitude.

Glossary

Calefactory – the "warming room", a gathering room for socialising, with a fireplace

Checker – small building in the abbey court where ledgers are kept and trades accounts are paid

Dorter – sleeping quarters

Frater – refectory

Office – communal devotions in chapel at intervals through the monastic day (for specifics, see "The Monastic Day" page)

Reredorter – literally, "behind sleeping quarters"; the toilets

The Community of St Alcuins Abbey

Monks in full profession

Abbot John Hazell (Father John)
Father Francis – prior
Father Theodore – novice master
Father Gilbert – precentor
Brother Cormac – cellarer
Father Dominic – guest-master
Father Bernard – sacristan
Father Gerard – almoner
Father Chad – librarian
Father James – robe maker, and helps in the scriptorium
Brother Thomas – abbot's esquire
Brother Michael – infirmarian
Brother Christopher – assistant infirmarian (Colin the postulant in earlier books)
Father William – assistant infirmarian
Brother Martin – porter
Brother Josephus – main school teacher
Brother Cassian – assistant school teacher
Brother Damian – helps in the school but mainly now works on the farm
Brother Stephen – oversees the farm work

Brother Placidus – helps on the farm
Brother Peter – ostler, and helps on the farm
Brother Conradus – kitchener
Brother Benedict – helps in the kitchen; occasionally co-opted for the infirmary
Brother Richard – fraterer, and does the laundry
Brother Walafrid – herbalist
Brother Giles – assistant herbalist and helps with the laundry
Brother Cedd – oversees the scriptorium
Brother Boniface – scribe
Brother Felix – scribe
Brother Thaddeus – potter
Brother Robert – assistant potter
Brother Germanus – oversees the garden work and orchards
Brother Mark – bee-keeper, now too old for other work
Brother Fidelis – does the flowers in the garth, now too old for other work
Brother Prudentius – helps in the kitchen garden, now too old for other work

Novices

Brother Anthony – (after Anthony the Great) works in the garden with Brother Germanus
Brother Nathaniel – (after the apostle) works on the farm
Brother Philip – (after the apostle) works in the scriptorium
Brother Ignatius – (after Ignatius of Antioch) works in the scriptorium
Brother Cyril – (after Cyril of Alexandria) just entered from being a postulant; his name used to be Rufus O'Conaill. Works in the kitchen, but also helps out with the horses and the laundry

Infirmary Residents

Father Clement – once oversaw the scriptorium
Father Paul – once precentor
Father Gerald – once sacristan
Brother Paulinus – once one of the gardeners
Brother Edward – once infirmarian. He was Abbot Columba's (Father Peregrine's) uncle
Brother Denis – once a scribe

Now deceased

Abbot Gregory of the Resurrection
Abbot Columba du Fayel (known as Father Peregrine)
Father Lucanus – once novice master
Father Matthew – once novice master
Father Aelred – once the schoolmaster
Father Ambrose – once cellarer
Father Anselm – once robe maker
Father Oswald – once an Augustinian
Brother Andrew – once kitchener
Brother Cyprian – once porter

The Monastic Day

There may be variation from place to place and at different times from the Dark Ages through the Middle Ages and onward – e.g. Vespers may be after supper rather than before. This gives a rough outline. Liberties are taken in my novels to allow human interactions to play out; and sometimes I just get it wrong.

Winter Schedule (from Michaelmas)

2:30am Preparation for the Nocturns of Matins – psalms, etc.
3:00am Matins, with prayers for the royal family and for the dead
5:00am Reading in preparation for
6:00am Lauds at daybreak and Prime; wash and break fast (just bread and water, standing)
8.30am Terce, the Morrow Mass, Chapter
12:00 noon Sext, sung (High) Mass, midday meal
2:00pm None
4:15pm Vespers, supper, Collatio
6:15pm Compline
The Grand Silence begins

Summer Schedule (from Easter)

1:30am Preparation for the Nocturns of Matins – psalms, etc.
2:00am Matins

3:30am Lauds at daybreak, wash and break fast
6:00am Prime, the Morrow Mass, Chapter
8:00am Terce, sung (High) Mass
11:30am Sext, midday meal
2:30pm None
5:30pm Vespers, supper, Collatio
8:00pm Compline
The Grand Silence begins

Timeline of *The Hawk and the Dove* stories

1259 Peregrine du Fayel is born in September.
1271 William is born.
1274 John is born.
1284 Peregrine enters monastic life at St Peters, Ely.
1285 Tom is born.
1288 William enters St Dunstans, aged 17.
1292 John enters St Alcuins, aged 18.
1303 Father Gregory of the Resurrection (Abbot of St Alcuins) dies. Peregrine becomes abbot aged 44 (turns 45 that year). William then 32. Two years pass.
1305 Tom enters, aged 20.
1306 (Lent) Peregrine disabled at age 47.
1307 Tom takes his solemn vows and becomes abbot's esquire.
1314 Peregrine mentions to Br. James in *The Wounds of God* how long he has been disabled.
1318 Peregrine is taken ill. Tom is 33 and has been his esquire for 11 years. Peregrine says he's worked 15 years to get the community back into solvency. He is 60 in the September of that year.
1318 Peregrine dies near the end of the year when he is 60.
1318 John is elected abbot and sent to Cambridge to be priested, then aged 44.
1320 In Lent John becomes abbot after 28 years in the community. William arrives. Madeleine arrives at Ascensiontide. William leaves right at the end of the year.

1322 William, married a year, comes back to visit in February when Father Ambrose dies.
1322 William comes back to help Brother Cormac in May.
1322 John has been in religion 30 years, abbot 2 years (is now 48). Tom is 37.
1325 Madeleine dies. William returns to St Alcuins in July. John has been in religion 33 years, abbot 5 years (is now 51). Tom is 40. William is 55.
1325 Brother Cyril writes his book.

1303 *The Hawk and the Dove*
1314 *The Wounds of God*
1318 *The Long Fall*
1320 (Lent) *The Hardest Thing to Do*
1320 (After Easter through to July) *The Hour Before Dawn*
1320 (August to December) *Remember Me*
1322 (February) *The Breath of Peace*
1322 (May) *The Beautiful Thread*
1323 (Summer) *A Day and a Life*
1325 (July and August) *This Brother of Yours*
1325 (September and October) *Brother Cyril's Book*

So, two full decades before the Black Death
1348 Plague comes to Britain.

The Ecclesiastical Year

I have included the main feasts and fasts in the cycle of the church year, plus one or two other important dates (e.g. Michaelmas and Lady Day when rents were traditionally collected) mentioned in the series.

Advent – begins four Sundays before Christmas
Christmas – December 25th
Holy Innocents – December 28th
Epiphany – January 6th
Baptism of our Lord concludes Christmastide, Sunday after January 6th
Candlemas – February 2nd (Purification of Blessed Virgin Mary, Presentation of Christ in the temple)
Lent – Ash Wednesday to Holy Thursday (start date varies with phases of the moon)
Holy Week – last week of Lent and the Easter Triduum
Easter Triduum (three days) of Good Friday, Holy Saturday, Easter Sunday
Lady Day – March 25th – this was New Year's Day between 1155 and 1752
Ascension – forty days after Easter
Whitsun (Pentecost) – fifty days after Easter
Trinity Sunday – Sunday after Pentecost
Corpus Christi – Thursday after Trinity

Sacred Heart of Jesus – Friday of the following week
Feast of John the Baptist – June 24th
Lammas (literally "loaf-mass"; harvest begins, barley first) – August 1st
Michaelmas – St Michael and All Angels, September 29th (harvest all gathered in)
All Saints – November 1st
All Souls – November 2nd
Martinmas – November 11th

Printed in the USA
CPSIA information can be obtained
at www.ICGtesting.com
LVHW041115280823
756502LV00024B/276

9 798374 27839